Brian C

INSIDE THE
GLOBE

TALES OF A 1940S BOYHOOD IN THE
NORTH OF ENGLAND

First published in paperback by
Michael Terence Publishing in 2023
www.mtp.agency

ISBN 9781800945432

Front Cover Illustration
Jodie Dowie

Michael Terence
Publishing

Contents

I wanted to ask Uncle Pip if he'd ever sailed to the side of the world - to the place where the sea met the sky. It was unlikely, I realised. He wouldn't have had the time, not with the war and having to stay with his gun day and night. I felt that a special expedition, something like Captain Scott's in a book Pete had, would be needed, sailing far out to the very extremities of the ocean. Only then might it be possible to bump against the sky as it rose majestically from the depths and soared upwards and far overhead in a great curved sheet. I could picture the explorers in rowing boats, able to prod the mysterious sky surface with their wooden oars, and maybe reach out a hand and touch *it…*

1
INSIDE THE GLOBE

"Yes it is!" I shouted.

"No it isn't!" Johnny Stone shouted back.

"It *is*, though!"

"It *can't* be!"

"The world is round! It is! Our *Pete* says so!"

That was the end of the matter, at least for the moment. Our Pete knew everything. He was three years older than Johnny and me, which seemed like a lifetime. He was going out into the world, far beyond the bottom end of Elderberry Lane, finding out stuff. He knew where to look, who to ask. Pete went to school. Johnny and I hadn't even started yet, because of the war. Pete was in Old Ma Handcart's class now. Her real name was Mrs Hankinson, but that was what everybody called her. Old Ma Handcart always wore trousers, and might have a wooden leg. She shouted a lot and some of the boys in the class were scared of her, but *he* wasn't.

Soon Pete would move up a class to join the big boys. Already he was going into their playground, talking to them. He knew all about the war and the different kinds of planes that were fighting to save our country - Spitfires, Hurricanes, Wellingtons, Lancasters, Mosquitoes. He had a book about them with lots of grey photographs. We never saw them in the skies over our house, though. What we did see were the planes from the nearby American base - great silver birds. Pete knew nearly all of *them*, too. And he could even name some of the *German* planes - Messerschmidts and Junkers and Fokkers. He said those names very seriously. Spitfires could shoot them all down, he reckoned. Dead easy.

But Pete was finding out lots of other stuff, too. He was always onto something new. One day he ran home from school to tell me what he'd found out only that morning.

"Heaven is all around us," he announced.

"Heaven?"

"The place you go to when you die."

Ours wasn't a religious home, but I *had* heard of the place. We had one grandma there already. Somewhere up above the clouds, it was. Or so I'd believed.

"We're in the middle of it right now, bumping into angels," Pete went on. "Only we don't know it."

"Why not?"

"Because they're *invisible*, that's why. A bit like ghosts."

"Do ghosts live there as well?"

"In heaven?"

"Yeah. Are we bumping into them, too?"

Pete looked thoughtful, but only for a second.

"I think ghosts only live in heaven at night," he said.

"What happens to them in the daytime?"

"They sleep, I think... I'll find out."

After that I walked around bumping into invisible angels for a while. It didn't matter that I couldn't feel them. I knew they were there because Pete had said they were. If anyone could get to the bottom of important stuff like that, *he* could. He was talking to the big boys every day, meeting them after school. Some of them were his pals.

But Pete didn't find out anything more about ghosts. Instead he told me next time he ran home from school that God had a first name.

"It's in a prayer we say in morning assembly," he said.

"What's a prayer?"

"It's when you speak to God. Sometimes you have to talk to him under your breath - without even moving your lips. But there's this one prayer the whole school says aloud. It's about trespassing."

"Trespassing? Going into the farmers' fields, you mean?"

"Yeah. Everybody seems to be doing it. But it's all right if they say they're sorry."

"Is God invisible - like the angels?"

"Yeah, but he's a *lot* scarier."

"What's his first name, anyway?"

"It's in the prayer about trespassing. *Hallow-ed*, it sounds like."

"That's a funny name."

"It might be *two* names…"

Pete usually told me things in secret, in our tiny back bedroom.

It was full of his stuff - half-built Meccano models and boys' adventure books and games like Snakes and Ladders and cigarette cards with smiling pictures of footballers on them and tin clockwork cars - all sorts of stuff like that. It was mostly pretty old, because you couldn't get much that was new with the war being on. He let me play with his stuff, but I was still a bit jealous. I didn't have much stuff of my own yet.

As soon as I got the chance I would dash round to my pal Johnny's house to tell him the latest news from Pete. Only I sometimes pretended it was something I'd found out for myself. He wouldn't believe me, though until I was forced to admit that it was really our Pete who'd told me. That was usually the end of it. But the day after our argument about whether the world was round or flat Johnny raised the matter again. I'd thought it was settled.

"How can it be round," he said, "when you can *see* it's flat?"

He pointed a finger all around. There was no denying what was in front of our eyes. It was my turn to look thoughtful.

"I don't know," I said. "Pete didn't explain it. He just told me that the world is round, that's all. I'll have to ask him about it again."

But next time Pete came into the bedroom and quietly closed the door, it was to tell me what he'd found out about babies and where they came from.

"Women get them in their stomachs somehow," he said, "and then when they're ready, they just *come out*."

"Through the *front*?"

"Yeah. Just like that."

"But don't they need an opening?"

"They don't seem to. It just seems to happen."

"Babies are quite *big*, though."

"Yeah, I know. Big enough nearly to fill a *pram*."

"Does the doctor or somebody have to use a knife?"

"I don't think so."

"How does it happen, then?"

"I'm not sure… I think it may have something to do with their belly buttons."

I could tell Pete didn't want me to ask any more questions about babies for now. He was happiest when he was just *telling* me stuff. But there was the other matter.

"You know when you said the world was round?"

"What?"

"The other day. You said the world was round."

"Yeah?"

"How *can* it be round? It looks *flat*."

He was silent for a moment.

"Well, it's sort of round and flat at the same time," he explained. "It *looks* flat, but it *is* round. That's all."

I tried to look as if I understood, which wasn't easy. I hoped there would be more explanation. Pete looked as if he might be thinking again, but then he said he was going out. He wanted to find out how the baby got into the woman's stomach in the first place. It wouldn't take him long he reckoned.

Round and flat at the same time - how could that *be*? It seemed impossible. But I remembered that Pete had also told me about a thing at school, up on top of a cupboard. It was a sort of model of the world, on a stand. A *globe*, Old Ma Handcart had once called it, though she hadn't lifted it down to show them properly. The world itself was also a globe, she'd explained. The globe on the cupboard was dusty and hard to see clearly, Pete said, but it seemed to be blue. And it was definitely *round*. No question about that. I thought about the round world and the flat ground we walked on for days. And then, lying in bed one morning after Pete had gone to school, the answer suddenly came into my head. From nowhere. Or maybe God put it there. Hallow-ed God. It certainly wasn't our Pete.

The world was like an enormous hollow blue-glass ball, filled to half way with land and sea. When we looked up at the curved blue sky we were really seeing the inside surface of this ball. This *globe*. But the land we *lived* on - across the middle - was flat, surrounded by sea. And the sea would lap up against the sky surface where they met - around the side. I almost smiled in bed. It wasn't impossible after all.

*****

"Remember Uncle Pip?" Pete asked me one day soon afterwards. "You know, in the navy? Mum and Dad are having a bit of a do for him when he comes home. A party, I think they mean. I heard them talking."

"Will it be his birthday?"

"No, it's because he'll be home for good. The war's nearly over."

Who could forget Uncle Pip? He had a great black beard, like the sailor on the Player's cigarette packet. I'd seen him when he was home on leave, in his sailor suit. The last time he'd swallowed three raw eggs, straight from the shell. He'd said that's how they had to eat them on his ship. They weren't allowed to leave their guns for a moment. They even *slept* propped up against them.

I suddenly had a thought.

"Has Uncle Pip sailed right across the sea?" I asked Pete.

"A big sea, yeah. It's called an ocean, I think."

This happened to be just what I wanted to hear.

"And does it stretch all the way across the world?"

"More or less, I think. Why?"

"Oh, nothing…"

I decided not to tell Pete any more, but to keep the idea to myself.

Then I'd be ahead of him for once. I wanted to ask Uncle Pip if he'd ever sailed to the side of the world - the place where the sea met the sky. It was unlikely, I realised. He wouldn't have had the time, not with the war and with having to stay with his gun day and night. I felt that a special expedition, something like Captain Scott's in a book Pete had, would be needed, sailing far out to the very extremities of the ocean. Only then might it be possible to bump against the sky as it rose majestically from the depths and soared upwards and far overhead in a great curved sheet. I could picture the explorers in rowing boats, able to prod the mysterious sky surface with their wooden oars, and maybe reach out a hand and *touch* it.

But perhaps Uncle Pip had at least glimpsed the sky in the

distance, through the mist, when he wasn't firing his gun. He might be able to tell me about *that*.

I don't know how I managed it, but I kept the question I was going to ask him secret as I waited for the party. He arrived as usual in his sailor suit, his beard blacker and bushier than ever. He was soon chatting to the other grown-ups, eating food without ever sitting down. Then he showed us his latest trick - tying a knot in a piece of string, in his *mouth*. You couldn't see what was happening, but you could tell his tongue and teeth were hard at work. It was really amazing, but for some reason I couldn't show that in my face. I felt sulky, somehow. Finally he crouched down and put an arm around me - which I tried to push away. I didn't like his great beard to come too close. Everyone could tell I had something I wanted to say to him, something of my own. This wasn't how I had imagined it at all, though - everybody listening intently. I thought my question was a very serious and grown-up one. But I knew now that they would probably all laugh no matter *what* I said, Pete included.

At last I had to say something.

"I want to know if you've ever sailed to the side of the world."

Despite feeling shy, I was desperate to know the answer. Uncle Pip tried to put his arm around me again, but I still didn't want him to.

He smiled anyway, though with his beard it was hard to see. It showed mainly in his eyes.

"You mean the *edge* of the world," he said gently. "But you can't reach it and fall off. Do you know why?"

"Yes," I said impatiently. "It's because the world is round. I *know* that."

"Well then, you can't sail to the edge, can you? It can't *have* an edge if it's round, can it?"

"I don't mean the edge, I mean the *side*. Have you ever sailed to the *side* of the world?"

Uncle Pip slowly stood up, the smile disappearing from his eyes.

"What's it *made* of, the side of the world?" I shouted up at him.

"Sky-blue glass, or what?"

Seeing that Uncle Pip was lost for an answer, Pete now stepped forward.

"The world is round!" he said, his face all red and angry. "I *told* you that!"

"I *know* it's round!" I was almost crying by this time. "We live inside it. I just want to know if Uncle Pip has ever sailed to the side of the world. To the *sky*. I want to know what the sky is made of. What it *feels* like."

But now even know-all Pete backed off. Uncle Pip turned away and said something quietly to someone, and in no time at all the kind of grown-up talk that leaves kids out had started up again. I was angry still, but I was just too small to insist on a serious answer to my very serious question. So I ran up to the bedroom instead.

I was surprised when a moment later Pete appeared. I expected him still to be angry, too, but he seemed already to have forgotten what had only just happened. He could be like that.

"I've found out," he said.

I didn't even want to speak to him.

"Found out what?"

"*You* know."

"Know what?"

"How the baby gets into the woman's stomach."

"Oh - *that.*"

"Yeah… It's sort of *weird*… What happens is…"

I waited, but something was stopping him telling me. He seemed to be struggling to picture in his mind whatever it was he was trying to describe. So I told him I didn't want to know anyway. Leaving him open-mouthed, I pushed past him and hurried downstairs again and out into Elderberry Lane to see Johnny.

On the way to his house, though, I stopped and looked up. A big American bomber was passing noisily overhead before coming in to land at the base, but it was the blue sky I was looking at, through the gaps in the clouds. I felt *my* mood changing. It did seem an awfully long way off. The glass globe must be absolutely *huge*…

My question to Uncle Pip had been stupid, I realised. An expedition to reach the sky, where it met the sea, would take more time than anyone could ever possibly spare. Maybe as much as a whole *lifetime.*

I decided not to tell Johnny what had happened.

And in future I wouldn't listen to a thing our Pete said. At least nobody had laughed.

2
OSCAR AND ANGELA

"They came on *horseback*. Some wore cowboy clothes and some wore headdresses with feathers and no shirts. They rode right past our gate, up to the base. The ones with feathers were *Indians*. I've seen them at the pictures."

Pete was telling me about when the Yanks had first arrived at the base to help us win the war. For me these suntanned young men in their smart uniforms had always been around, hurrying down Elderberry Lane to the bus stop on the main road. But he could remember them coming. Or so he said.

"Why do we call them Yanks?" I asked him.

"Yanks? 'Cause they're Americans."

"Why don't we just call them *Americans*, then?"

"Yanks is the same thing."

"It's a different word, though."

"Well, they're Yanks, that's all. *All* Americans are Yanks."

"Oh."

We'd reached one of those moments again when he didn't want me to ask any more questions. It kept happening, even though I never set out deliberately to try to annoy him. I just wanted to know.

"So do they still wear feathers and stuff?" I asked instead.

"Sometimes up at the base they do. But when they come out

they have to put on their uniforms. That's so the English people won't be scared of them. Up there, though, they have these big fights and fire their bows and arrows at each other. Or *guns* if they're cowboys. They never bring their horses off the base, either. Cowboys are the goodies."

"Have they got *horses*?"

"Sure."

"Couldn't they use them to ride into town, then?"

Pete frowned.

"There wouldn't be anywhere to tie the horses up, would there?" he said. "So it's probably a lot easier for them to use the bus."

"How can you tell the cowboys from the Indians, when they're all in uniform?"

He thought again for a moment.

"Well, you can't," he said. "The uniforms are a disguise. They've *got* to wear them. They can only fight in their cowboys-and-Indians clothes up at the base. I expect they'd be put in prison if they tried to do it in town."

"What's the base *like*, anyway?"

I hadn't been up there yet myself yet. It was somewhere up beyond the point where the houses ended and the lane curved maddeningly out of sight.

"Mostly it's huts for them to sleep in. But sometimes they're outside in the sun, lying on the grass reading comics. Behind the wire fence."

"When do they fight, then?"

"After they've had an argument or something, I expect. Same as at the pictures."

I hadn't yet been to the pictures, either. You had to be old enough to go into town. Pete was always talking about what he'd seen. He went on Saturday mornings with some of his older pals, when it was nearly always a cowboy film.

I talked to Johnny about all this later, as usual. He said it sounded a bit screwy to him.

"My Auntie Gwen works up at the base," he told me. "She goes on a special bus. She never says anything about horses. All they've got up there are *aeroplanes*."

"Well, there could be horses *and* aeroplanes."

"But what are the horses *for*?"

"The Yanks ride them, when they're not flying their planes. Like Pete says. They fight on *horseback*."

But I could see that Johnny still didn't believe any of it, and it was beginning to seem a bit screwy to me, too. I was always making up my mind not to listen to Pete. Then I'd forget.

Just at that moment we heard the rumble and roar of another huge silver bomber in the sky. It passed so low over our heads that we thought our ears might burst.

"What do you think it is?" Johnny shouted through the din.

"A Flying Fortress, I expect. I'll ask Pete. He knows all about planes."

But Pete was never ready to talk about what I wanted to talk about. With him it had to be something new, and just lately he was starting to pick up the Yankee lingo, as he called it.

"Howdy pardner," he said, when next he caught me alone in our bedroom. He was moving his mouth in a funny way, I noticed. Sort of chewing. "Hey, I know this great guy."

I didn't know what a guy was. I thought he meant Guy Fawkes or somebody.

"Is he real?"

"Real? Sure he's real."

"But isn't he *stuffed*. Didn't we put Guy Fawkes on the bonfire on Bonny Night?"

"No, this is a proper guy. His name's Gus."

"Gus Guy?"

"No, just Gus. He's a Yank. A *cowboy*, I think."

"How did you meet him?"

"Up at the base. He was lying on the grass with the others, reading comics. Gus says he'll have some *great* ones for me soon. He's already given me some gum."

"Gum? What's that?"

He stopped chewing and brought something out of his mouth. It looked like a bit of wet grey plasticine.

"Want a chew?"

I put it in my mouth. It didn't taste of anything at all. The flavour had all gone.

"*Great*, isn't it?" said Pete.

"Yeah," I said, handing it quickly back.

But the next time he went up to see Gus at the base he came back with chocolate bars. They had names like *Hershey* and *Baby Ruth*. Pete read out the names on the wrappers.

"Have some *candy*," he said.

This was more like it - the best thing I'd ever tasted. I waited for him to say something else while I enjoyed it.

"Gus asked me if I had an older sister, or if any of my buddies had one."

"Why did he want to know that?"

Pete frowned.

"I think they need them to do their washing and stuff."

He suddenly dug into the pocket of his short trousers and brought out a small green and silver packet.

"Hey, I found this as well. It was in the long grass."

"What is it?"

"*Silver-Tex*," he read slowly, examining the fancy print. "More gum I think."

He tore open the packet and instead began pulling out a peculiar rubbery thing.

"What's *that*?"

"I think it's a… one of them… you know." He pulled a slight face and pushed the thing carefully back.

"But *what*?"

"A *Silver-Tex*, like I said."

"But what's it *for*?"

Pete frowned again. He was doing it a lot lately.

"I'll ask Gus."

When I next saw Johnny I'd forgotten all about the funny rubbery thing in the packet. Instead I told him what we had to do to get gum and candy off the Yanks coming down Elderberry lane. According to Pete, all you had to do was ask:

"Any *gum* chum?"

They were always in a rush to get to the bus stop, so the best thing, he reckoned, was to try to hold them up. Then the Yank would rummage quickly through his pockets to see what he could find. And Pete was right for once. It was dead easy, we found, when we tried it. Their pockets would be *bulging*. They didn't seem to know what they had in them half the time, so it was no bother for them to hand out gum and candy and stuff. Or if they were really in a hurry they'd just drop it on the ground, then step over us while we scrabbled about on our knees.

They never asked about older sisters when they were going down to the bus stop. That would happen when they were coming back up the lane, on their way home to the base. They walked a lot more slowly then and sometimes staggered about. Pete reckoned they were usually drunk, but I wasn't sure what he meant. They looked sad to me.

Johnny and I quickly realised they could be even more generous going home, though. All you had to do was *hint* that there was an older sister hidden away in one of the houses - even though there weren't any to speak of - and they would empty their pockets.

I was beginning to think that Pete must be onto something like this, too. He was coming back from the base with better stuff now, including the Yankee comics his friend Gus had promised. The only comics we'd seen were cheap, skimpy English ones, like the *Dandy* or the *Knockout,* badly printed on thin paper that you could see through. Gus was giving Pete fat, glossy, full-colour comics with names like *Captain Marvel* and *Superman* and *Batman.* I still hadn't started school, so I couldn't read even the titles very well, but it was easy to see how wonderful they were.

Pete soon had a great stack of them in our bedroom, which he could swap with his older pals for all kinds of things.

"Doesn't Gus ever pass this way on his way into town?" I asked him one day.

"Not walking. He drives a jeep. He probably goes past in that and we never notice him."

"Will he stop some time, though?" I was beginning to want to meet Gus myself.

"He wouldn't know where we live."

"Why don't you tell him?"

Pete looked worried. It was more than a frown.

"I almost did last time I went up to the base. I'm scared, though. I've told him I've got this cousin who's seventeen and sometimes comes to our house. Angela, I've said she's called. She's got blonde hair."

"But all our cousins are *boys.*"

"I know. He isn't interested in them. It's *Angela* he wants to meet.

I'm having to put him off. I may have to stop going up there."

A week or so later, when Pete was at school and I was playing alone with a ball close to our house, I saw a jeep speeding down Elderberry Lane.

Normally you had to be quick to get out of their way, but to my surprise this one screeched to a halt and a Yank jumped out. He was smoking a cigarette and had on a leather jacket and a cap with a badge.

"Hey, buddy," he called, tilting back his cap. "You know a kid named Pete, lives around these parts some place?"

"Pete? Yeah, he's my *brother*." I stopped bouncing the ball.

"Well ain't that somethin', pardner." He grinned, bending a little, his hands on his knees. "Is he home? Could I speak with him?"

"He's at school today. Are you *Gus*?"

"I sure am. Hey, is your sister in the house?"

"I haven't got a sister."

He sucked at the cigarette, straightening up.

"You sure, kid?"

"Yeah, I've only got a brother. That's Pete."

"Who's this *Angela* dame, then?"

I didn't like telling lies, but there was nothing else for it. I wasn't going to lose a chance like this to get to know Gus better.

"Oh, she's only our cousin. She doesn't live here."

"Close by, though, hey?"

"Not really. Though not *too* far away."

"Will she be coming by?"

"Soon, I expect."

"You mean today, kid?"

"No, not today. *Tomorrow*, maybe. Or *one* day."

"God damn it!" he said, almost under his breath. I thought he might jump back in his jeep and zoom off, but he hesitated.

"Hey, what happened to Pete, anyhow?" he asked.

"Pete? He's OK."

"I don't *see* him now."

I couldn't think of anything to say, so I didn't try. Gus sucked harder at his cigarette, deep in thought. Then he said:

"Can I fix *you* up with somethin', kid? Maybe *we* can be buddies."

It was just what I'd been hoping for. And I knew straight away what I wanted from Gus. Chocolate bars and stuff were easy to get now, and comics weren't of much use to me yet."

"Do you mean *anything*?"

"Sure, kid."

I gave the ball a bounce.

"Could I have a *white mouse*?"

"A *what*?"

I said it again. A white mouse was the thing I wanted more than anything else in the world just then. I'd seen one in a pet shop, in town with my mum.

He pulled a face but said, "Well, I'll *try*, kid."

More time passed and I was beginning to think Gus must have forgotten but then one day when Pete was at school again his jeep came racing up. He jumped out and rummaged in the back. I ran to see what he'd brought. He lifted out a small wooden cage, painted yellow and blue, with a little door. Over the door was a name, and inside was a real white mouse, with pink eyes and a twitchy nose.

"Wow!" I said.

"Like it, kid?"

"Yeah! What does *that* say?" The name was a bit faded, but you could still make out the letters.

"Ain't you readin' yet? It says *Oscar.*"

"Who's Oscar?"

"Who's *Oscar*? Why, Oscar is your new little buddy. You *did* say you wanted a mouse, didn't you, kid?"

"Yeah! Thanks Gus!" He handed me the cage, dusting off his hands as if he was glad to be rid of it.

"Is Angela visiting today?" he asked, after a pause.

"Angela? Not today, Gus."

"Are you expecting her?"

I was trying to take a closer look at the mouse. "We never

know when she's coming," I told him, avoiding his eyes.

"Will you give her a message from me?"

I nodded, half expecting him to hand me a piece of paper, but he just said, "Tell her I'd like to *meet* her sometime. I'll bring her some nylons and stuff."

"Have you got *washing* that needs doing?"

"Washing? Hell no." He scratched his head under his cap and climbed back into his jeep.

"Tell her what I said, now! Don't you forget!"

"OK Gus."

When Pete came home I showed him the mouse and told him what had happened. He seemed more worried than excited.

"Did you tell him where we live?"

"No, but he may have guessed."

"Don't you ever dare talk to him again!"

"Why not?"

"Because it's *Angela* he's interested in, and there *is* no Angela. He may want all the comics and stuff *back*."

But I thought Pete was only jealous - because Gus had given me something better than the stuff he'd given him.

"I'm going to ask for another mouse," I told him. "Oscar should have a little buddy."

"If you do that, I'll *kill* him."

"Kill *who*?"

"Oscar."

So I took the mouse round to Johnny's. I knew his mum and dad wouldn't mind. They already had rabbits and guinea pigs. At first we were excited about the mouse and spent a lot of time with it. But the trouble was, it didn't do anything except scamper about in its cage a bit, sometimes eating and sometimes doing something else. It was the something else we got tired of first. Johnny's dad made us clean out the cage every day.

Meanwhile it wasn't long before Gus called again. Pete was at home this time, but he ran and hid in the bedroom. He told me to follow, but I wasn't quick enough.

"Is the mouse OK?" Gus asked.

"Yeah. Fine."

"Eating OK?"

"Sure."

"Drinking?"

I nodded.

"Sleeping?"

"Yeah, I think so."

Gus lit a cigarette. He was still sitting in the jeep, sort of nervous.

"Angela home? Did you give her my message?"

"I haven't seen her since. She doesn't live here."

"Oh yeah. So you said."

He threw the cigarette away, even though there was a lot left, and drove off. I picked it up and ran indoors and up to the bedroom. I knew Pete would be angry so I handed him the cigarette, which was still lit.

"Gus gave me this."

He took it from me, sucked at it, then coughed a lot.

"Just don't talk to him again!" he said. "OK?"

"OK."

But I knew it wouldn't be easy. I wanted that second mouse as a friend for Oscar so that Johnny and I wouldn't have to spend so much time with him. We were pretty fed up of the mouse by this time. But Gus didn't call again for a while. One sunny afternoon we decided to let it play in the fresh air. We carried the cage onto the lawn at the back of the house and opened the door.

The mouse was scared at first, but he sniffed the air then stepped hesitantly onto the grass. There was a little drop, but he landed on his feet OK. At that point, though, he seemed to run out of ideas. We watched him for a bit, then we started talking about other things.

Suddenly I saw that he was gone.

"Where's *Oscar*?" I cried.

Johnny was looking at my feet.

"Just *behind* you, I think."

I hardly dared look. When I did I saw that Oscar was lying on the grass, perfectly still.

"Oscar! What do you think is *wrong* with him?"

"I think you must have *trodden* on him," said Johnny.

"Me? Why me?"

"Well, maybe it was me."

"Is he *dead?*"

Johnny turned the mouse over with his toe.

"Dead as a doornail."

But the funny thing was, neither of us seemed to care very much.

Johnny brought a trowel from the shed after a while and we dug a little hole and dropped the mouse into it. Then we filled in the hole with earth and stamped it down. The whole thing took us about five seconds. We were left with the cage, but we didn't care about that, either.

A few days later Gus called again. This time he was in a car, a huge blue one - very flashy. He had the window down and the engine running still. I wanted to say something about it, but he spoke first.

"How's Oscar?" he shouted.

"I *trod* on him," I shouted back.

"You did *what?*"

"It was an accident."

"Oh, well I'm sorry to hear that, kid. I truly am."

Gus stopped the car's engine. He seemed on the point of lighting a cigarette as usual, but then changed his mind. He pushed his cap up off his forehead.

"So I guess I ain't ever gonna meet no Angela dame, huh, kid?"

I shook my head, staring hard at the ground.

There was a silence.

"Like some gum, buddy?" he sighed at last.

"Sure thing!"

I could see him digging around in the pocket of his leather jacket.

Then he pulled out a green and silver packet. He held it in the palm of his hand for a moment, pulling a face. Then he stuffed it quickly back and tried again.

3

THE BARMPOT AND THE PAINT JOB

We didn't see many *English* cars on Elderberry Lane, though a few families had them. The cars were old, squeezed onto bits of land alongside the houses. The tyres would be mostly flat, with the wheels sometimes twisted at crazy angles. One or two would have broken windows as well, letting the rain in to damage the leather seats that we could see inside if we sneaked a look. These English cars were black, but not *shiny* black, the way they must once have been. Now they were just dull, like the fences, side gates and trellises. Nobody had had any paint for years because of the war. I'd never seen one of the old cars move, and couldn't imagine it happening.

Pete reckoned they'd always been that way, since even before the Yanks came.

"The people bought them just for show," he told me one day, while he was trying to mend a clockwork car in our bedroom.

"To go to the pantomime, you mean? *That* show?" He'd been on a school trip to see *Dick Whittington* at the theatre in town. That was ages ago, back in the winter, when there was snow on the ground. We were now in spring, though he still talked about it sometimes.

"No - to show *off*," he said.

"Oh." I felt stupid for a moment. "But how can they do that, if the cars never move?"

"Just by *having* them. Cars cost a lot of money."

"Where do they get that from - money?"

"From banks. That's where all the money's kept. Some people can just go into a bank and then walk away with pound notes in their hands. I've seen them in town, counting the notes as they go off down the street. The banks won't give just anyone money, though."

"Why not?"

"Well, they've only got so much. If they were giving money all the time to everybody they'd soon have none left, wouldn't they?"

"Couldn't *we* get some?"

"No."

"Why not?"

"I went in a bank one day to ask."

This was just like Pete. Sometimes I thought he must be making it all up. But you could *half* believe the things he said, so you had to keep on asking questions, even if it sometimes annoyed him. As he talked he kept turning the key of the clockwork car, frowning now and then. He wasn't having any luck, though. The spring had gone. Even *I* knew that. It was always happening with things you had to wind up.

"Why don't the cars ever move, anyway, like the American ones?"

Important Yanks like Gus were now riding up and down the lane in their Chevrolets and Oldsmobliles and Plymouths. Pete knew all the names. Not only were the Yankee cars enormous, a lot of them were coloured, like Gus's, instead of black. We'd even seen a *pink* one.

"The English cars haven't got engines any more," Pete explained.

That's what the trouble is. They had to have them taken out for the war. To put in the aeroplanes."

I thought of chasing round to Johnny's house with this latest news, but I knew he'd only argue. And in fact a day or two later Pete explained it differently.

"It's *petrol* the cars need," he said. "You can't drive them without it.

They won't go."

"What's that - petrol?"

"It's what makes the engines work. Only special people can have it, and then only about a cupful."

"Which people?"

"The same ones who can get money from a bank, I expect."

But the spring turned into summer, the war against Germany was suddenly over at last - and then we noticed something surprising. The car owners were now getting a few cupfuls of petrol from somewhere, because the rusted old cars of Elderberry Lane were starting to stir. We saw one or two actually move a short distance up and down the lane. Some had even been given a fresh coat of black paint by their owners, too. But they were other people's cars, and not really very interesting to us. In fact cars of any kind or colour seemed to have no connection whatever with *our* lives...

And then Johnny and I were hanging around at the bottom of Elderberry Lane one sunny afternoon, waiting for something to happen, when we saw an older boy we hardly knew coming towards us - from nowhere. We didn't even know where he lived, but we knew *about* him. I'd heard my mum refer to him as *Caldwell's lad.* He didn't seem to have a first name. He stole things, everyone said, and was going to end up in the Naughty Boys' School before he was much older, if he wasn't careful. He didn't *look* particularly naughty, though - just sort of goofy-looking, with sticky-out ears and teeth, and hair combed straight forward. I'd seen him climbing trees. Not trees in the woods, though. He liked climbing them in people's gardens. Pete said he was a *barmpot.* He had no friends and wandered around our neighbourhood and other places always on his own.

"I'm on my way to help Mrs Stringer to do some painting," he said importantly. "Coming?"

"What? You mean *Billy* Stringer's mother?"

"That's right."

Well, he was a bit smaller than us, but we knew Billy. He lived in a big house down on the main road - one of those that you somehow never got to see the inside of. There were other families like that - the Sherburns, for instance. They had a spoiled only child, David, who had *everything* but wouldn't let you touch *anything.* And then there were rough families with lots of kids like the Quarrys - way up at the top of the lane. You kept away from houses like theirs. But *Billy* was all right, even if his parents were a bit snobby. They had a car, and even a garage. Their car had been locked away while the war was on, but now we often saw it standing out on the concreted bit at the side of the house. It still looked old and sad, though.

"Why *Mrs* Stringer?" Johnny asked. It seemed strange that she was going to do the painting job, whatever it was.

Caldwell's lad shrugged his shoulders.

"But what about *Mr* Stringer?" We didn't like the man. He had a terrible temper. We'd seen him give Billy a good hiding more than once for almost nothing. He didn't care *who* was watching.

"Don't be stupid! He'll be at *work*."

"Oh."

Johnny ran out of questions at this point, although maybe he was feeling scared of the boy all of a sudden. I know I was. Caldwell's lad didn't look nearly so goofy when you got up close. There was definitely something that wasn't quite right about him. I couldn't understand how he'd managed to get himself involved in whatever it was that was being planned. It was a surprise to me that he even knew who Billy Stringer *was*. But like Johnny, I said nothing.

"Are you coming, then, or what?" he said impatiently.

We didn't answer, but obediently followed him. To get to Stringer's house you had to cross the main road. Our new friend ran straight across without looking. We were a bit more careful, although there wasn't much traffic and it hardly seemed necessary. I hoped that Mrs Stringer and Billy would be out in the garden on such a fine day, but they were nowhere to be seen. It didn't put Caldwell's lad off, though. He casually lifted the latch of the gate and marched boldly up to the front door. We followed more nervously. He tried ringing the bell a few times, then banged loudly on the knocker.

No one came.

"Funny," he said.

Still very bold, he led us around to the back door, which in fact was at the side of the house, with a little porch. He entered this, then knocked loudly with his fist on the door inside. Still no one came.

"Funny," he said again, shielding his eyes from the sun as he peered through a side window.

"We'd better go," I said, in a loud whisper.

"No, it's OK. Honest. She said we should start without her. I know where everything is, and the car's out already."

"What's the *car* got to do with it?"

"It's the car we're *painting.*"

"Oh," Johnny and I said together.

Opening the garage doors wide, Caldwell's lad pointed to some big tins on a high shelf. We could see dry bright orange paint where it had run down the sides.

"Fetch me those stepladders!" he commanded.

Johnny and I dragged them across the rough concrete floor. He quickly set them up and climbed to the top, then handed the tins down to us one by one.

"Now we need brushes."

"Where will we get *them* from?"

There was only a moment's hesitation.

"On that bench over there!"

And there they were, three or four lined up ready for use, and more in a jam jar. They weren't terribly clean and the bristles were all stiff and bent, but they seemed perfect to us. Soon we had the paint tins out in the sunshine, with the lids prised off.

"Shouldn't we wait for Mrs Stringer to come?" Johnny asked, though we already knew the answer.

"I *told* you. There's no need."

Caldwell's lad carried his tin to the front end of the car and dipped his brush deep into the tempting orange liquid.

"Where shall *we* paint?"

"You two can start at the back."

We positioned ourselves one at each corner, ready for the order to begin, feeling suddenly excited.

"OK, let's start painting!"

Johnny and I only dabbed at the car at first, but when we saw the older boy starting to slosh the stuff on we set to work. You didn't have to be any good at it. You just painted everything in sight.

The tyres were a problem, we soon found out, because you couldn't paint the part that was touching the ground. And we were disappointed to find we couldn't reach the roof, except around the edges. Otherwise it was easy, although Johnny complained that the window he was painting was streaky because his brush had lots of bristles missing. But that was no problem. Our leader agreed to swap with him. He'd already finished *his* windows.

"Does she want the glass painting on the inside as well?" we asked.

We'd discovered that the doors weren't locked.

"She didn't say, but I think we'd better."

Well, the sun shone, the birds sang in the trees, and we lost ourselves completely in the delicious task. Had we been able to, we would have whistled merrily... But then something happened. We were well into our second coat when I sensed that we were no longer alone.

Glancing across at the house back door, I was startled to see that Mrs Stringer and Billy had appeared. How they'd got there I didn't know, but they were standing silently outside the porch. I paused in my painting, waiting for our leader to speak. Time seemed to freeze. I felt sure that a word from him would quickly put right whatever had gone wrong, but he stayed silent, too.

Then he dropped his brush and ran for it.

It only took Johnny and me a moment longer to realise the enormity of what we had done. By the time we reached the gate, though, all we could see of Caldwell's lad were the orange skid marks he'd left along the pavement, veering off towards the main road.

"Where shall we *go*?" I said, as we began running for our lives.

"Home!" said Johnny.

"But we'll get *killed*!"

"I know. But there's nowhere *else*."

I was lucky that my good and worldy-wise Auntie Jessie happened to be visiting - a rare thing.

34

"Get in that bathroom quick, before your mother sees the state of you!" she shouted, shoving me in that direction.

"I *told* you, Caldwell's a barmpot!" Pete said later - after the fathers had spent hours scrubbing the car with turps, and after the police had called, and after bad-tempered Mr Stringer had calmed down at last, and Mum had at last begun to talk about other things.

I wasn't even sure what he meant.

"Didn't I tell you he once broke into a lorry and ran it down a slope into a wall? They nearly locked him away for *that*. And then he climbed into somebody's bedroom from a tree in the garden and stole jewellery and stuff. The police always catch him, but he can't *stop* himself."

Some of the things the naughty boy had done might have tempted Pete himself, I thought, but he could sound just like a grown-up when he was in the mood. Or a *teacher* - I'd just started school after the summer holidays. I was still puzzled about how the boy had known exactly where the paint and brushes and stuff were, while Dad was more interested in where Mr Stringer had got the paint *from*. But those were questions that would never be answered.

Caldwell's lad didn't remain a barmpot for long. Nor was he ever sent to the Naughty Boys' School. One day soon afterwards Mum was slowly turning the pages of the local *Reporter* at the kitchen table, as she did every weekend, when she suddenly let out a cry. For a moment she couldn't speak.

"That *boy*!" she gasped. "He's been run over by a bus, on the other side of town somewhere. Ran straight across the road, it says. Didn't give the driver a chance. Killed instantly."

4
PLEASE MISS!

"Ever noticed there aren't many girls around here?" Pete asked me one day.

"Girls? No."

Who was interested in *girls*?

"They've all been taken away somewhere," he explained, frowning. "Stolen, maybe."

"*Stolen*?"

"That's right. Like in a poem Old Ma Handcart read to us once. It was about a man in funny clothes who played beautiful music on a pipe, and the children of the town couldn't stop themselves following him. He'd had this big row with the other grown-ups, so he led all the children off to a faraway place in the country, playing on his pipe, and they were never seen or heard of again."

While he talked, I tried to think of the girls living on Elderberry Lane.

Pete was right, there were hardly any. I hadn't thought about it before.

It was possible that a few girls were kept indoors, higher up the lane, a territory ruled by the Quarry family, though you never saw them walking down to the bus stop, not even with their mums. Otherwise I could only think of little Malcolm Bailey's big sister Mary, and we hardly ever saw her. She had to stay indoors for some reason. So that left only the *Quarry* girls and they hardly counted. They were a family mainly of boys, but the girls might just as well have been. They had the same short haircuts and red, screwed-up faces, and they fought just as hard. The youngest, their Barb, was the scariest, although their Sam, a bit older, was someone to avoid as well. And that was about it for girls. It would have been difficult for us to introduce the Yanks to one of any age, unless you went all the way up to *Gert* Quarry, who was more or less grown up. But Gert was even scarier than Barb. She would have frightened the poor Yanks to death.

"A pipe?" I said, noticing that Pete had stopped talking about the poem. "You mean like a pipe for smoking?"

We had a granddad who had a whole rack of pipes. Grandma - the one who wasn't yet up in heaven - would choose a different one for him to smoke when he got home from work, while he sat in his rocking chair. That was after she'd struggled to pull off his boots. He had a hard job, carrying goods around the town from the station with a big cart and a team of horses.

"No," Pete said. "This kind of pipe you played music on."

I tried to imagine what it might look like.

"And did the man only steal the girls of the town?" I asked.

"Girls *and* boys, I think."

"So why didn't that happen here? Why have only the *girls* been stolen."

"Well, it was *different* here. Nobody played any music, or anything like that. The girls were taken to safe, faraway places in buses, that's all.

It was because of the war. Everybody was worried about the bombs that were going to be dropping out of the sky."

"But why were the boys left behind? Did nobody care if the bombs dropped on *us*?"

"No one knew how long the war was going to last, so I expect they thought boys might be needed to fight one day. Once we were grown up and everything."

"But when will the girls be coming back?"

"They ought to be back *now*. I heard a man talking on the wireless. *Evacuees*, he called them. Most of them went to places by the sea. The buses should be bringing them home any day."

But I kept watching for buses, and the missing girls never did come home to Elderberry Lane. You rarely saw even a day-trip charabanc up there. I didn't think any of this was worth mentioning to Johnny.

At school it was much the same, I began to notice. There weren't nearly so many girls as boys. It made them seem more special, and we already knew from a nursery rhyme we kept hearing that they were made from better things than we were. *Sugar and spice and all things nice…* They wore pretty frocks, these special creatures, with coloured ribbons in their hair. Their hands and faces were always spotlessly clean, too, and they wouldn't have any scabs on their knees. It was all new to me - and a bit scary.

I mean the girls were so good at their schoolwork as well. Some of them even did homework, without being *told* to. They seemed to have started school knowing how to write and do sums already. And when they wrote in chalk on the little slates we were given, or later in pencil in tiny exercise books, it was all so very neat and perfect that as a boy you felt you should be outdoors climbing trees or jumping in mud. School was a place for *girls*. No doubt about it.

Another special thing about them was that they didn't often have to leave the room in the middle of a lesson. Most of them, anyway. But there was one girl who *did*. All the time. That was Beryl Fitchett. Beryl wasn't much like the other girls, for some reason. She was tall and thin, with a pointed nose that was usually red and wet-looking, and long hair that was never tied with ribbons or held up in any other way. Sometimes it hung like a curtain right across her face. That would be when she was trying to write, with her wet nose about an inch from the paper. When we moved on from little chairs round a table to bigger, two-seater desks - in Miss Nearhoof's class - it was my bad luck to have to share one with Beryl.

No one liked her much, not even Miss Nearhoof, who as a rule definitely preferred girls. Her great favourite was Susan Granger. She was the *boys'* favourite, too.

It was Beryl's need to use the toilet so often that most annoyed Miss Nearhoof. Some of the boys could be more of a nuisance than she was, but they would be shouted at and sometimes slapped on the legs before leaving the room, and that would be the end of it. Girls weren't supposed to need to go, apparently. I don't think Susan Granger *ever* went, even at playtime. But poor Beryl couldn't help herself.

She was often late for school, missing morning assembly. Why that was I never found out, but she would eventually arrive in the seat beside me, red-faced and out of breath. It would take her ages to settle down but then the other business would start.

I would wait in dread for the first tiny movements.

At first they weren't very noticeable, so that I could believe nothing much was happening. But then her knee would brush against mine. I'd try hard to think of something or somebody else - such as golden-haired Susan Granger, who always wore the prettiest frocks and ribbons and had the nicest smile and could sing like an angel and was said to be having piano lessons. The point would soon come, though, when Beryl's long legs could no longer be ignored. I would try edging along the seat, out of their range, but soon her bony knee would find mine again as the opening and closing of her legs built up to desperation pitch.

What made it all the more alarming was that I hadn't a clue how girls' bodies worked. I guessed they were not equipped as we were with an obvious means of relieving themselves, if the toilet could be reached in time. But what took its place I couldn't imagine. Even Pete hadn't yet got to the bottom of that one, though he was keen to find out. Sometimes I feared that Beryl might have no choice but to *explode*.

Long before our desk had begun to shake and rattle, the rest of the class would know what was happening and would have started to giggle. Only stupid Miss Nearhoof always failed to notice Beryl's desperation - until the painful moment at last came when the poor girl could wait no longer and had no alternative but to raise her hand.

"Yes, Beryl - what *is* it?" our teacher would snap.

"Please may I leave the room, Miss?"

"Certainly *not*."

"*Please* Miss?"

"No."

"But *Miss…*"

"I said *no*, Beryl. You must learn to *control* yourself. Now, where were we?"

Miss Nearhoof would do her best to go on with the lesson, but Beryl would have to raise her hand again almost immediately.

"Please Miss, I've *got* to."

"*No*, Beryl."

The rest of the class would be giggling once more - but not Susan Granger, whose nose would be raised in a superior way. Sometimes she would turn and glare at Beryl - or as it appeared to me, at both of us. It seemed that Susan disapproved of Beryl's lack of control just as strongly as the teacher did.

"Be quiet, everyone!" Miss Nearhoof would shout, lifting her huge chest off the high desk on which it usually rested, so that it swayed from side to side. What she had *in* there was as big a mystery to me as the girls' equipment for relieving themselves.

Here Susan might raise her hand.

"Please Miss, my mum says we shouldn't have all these interruptions in class. She says it interferes with our education."

"And your mother is right, Susan."

As my desk companion approached her climax of agony, my own feelings would be in turmoil. Like all the boys in the class, I secretly adored Susan Granger, and was always ready to excuse her goody-goody ways.

And I hated Beryl Fitchett. If I'd been sitting anywhere else

I'd have joined in the rising mockery. But being so close, I could *feel* Beryl's pain. I alone in the classroom understood the terrible unfairness of it all. And by now I would have begun to imagine that I might soon need to go myself. Miss Nearhoof's mood made me want to avoid that at all costs.

Finally, the girl would have no choice but to stand up and begin to leave the room *without* permission.

"Beryl! Sit down at once!" Miss Nearhoof would command, getting to her feet.

But Beryl would have to press on, bursting into tears as she reached for the doorknob. It was a moment I really couldn't stand. Miss Nearhoof would seem to be on the point of chasing after the girl, to give her legs a really *good* slapping, to teach her a lesson once and for all. But thankfully she never did. Later, though, she might keep Beryl behind at playtime, or even after school, and she had other little ways of punishing her.

In the playground one day, Beryl Fitchett surprised me by *speaking* to me.

Normally we kept a silence, whether outdoors or in. Miss Nearhoof and Susan Granger had been giving her a worse time than ever. I was leaning against the wall, one foot raised, thinking of other things. I hadn't noticed Beryl edging up to me, even though she was about six inches taller than I was.

"I'm going to *kill* that Susan Granger," she suddenly said, in a loud whisper. Her nose was redder and wetter than ever, but there was a hard look in her eye that I hadn't seen before.

"What?"

"Susan Granger. I'm going to *kill* her. Just *look* at her!"

Susan was standing a short distance away, surrounded by some of the more adventurous boys. I had been wondering how they'd found the courage to approach her so closely. Two of the boys were even *talking* to her.

"*Kill* her, did you say?"

"Yes, and you've got to help me."

I laughed. "Why should I?"

"Because if you don't, I'm going to go over there and tell her you're *potty* about her."

"But you can't do *that*!"

Nothing could have terrified me more. I knew that if Beryl carried out her threat, I'd have to die myself.

"Just *watch* me!"

And without hesitating she left my side and began to walk straight towards Susan and her little group of admirers. I rushed after her, pulling at her sleeve.

"Beryl - don't! *Please*! I'll *help* you."

"Good," she said, moving back towards the wall. "Now, what I want you to do is crouch down behind her, so I can push her over. It'll be dead easy."

"But *that* won't kill her."

"It will if she bangs her head hard on the concrete. Her skull will be cracked, and I'll see all the blood and everything coming out."

You wouldn't have guessed that Beryl could *have* such

thoughts.

"But she'll *see* me, in any case."

"No she won't. You can pretend you're just tying your shoelace or something. You can bet she'll be too interested in the other boys, though, to notice *you*."

"But *Beryl*..."

"Go on!" she said, when I continued to stand there.

To avoid being pushed, I set off. I made my way slowly in a big circle, until Susan had her back to me. Then, inch by inch, I moved in behind her. No one had paid me the slightest attention so far. I bent down on one knee and examined one of my shoelaces. Out of the corner of my eye I saw Beryl straighten her arms, clench her fists, and begin to stride towards her enemy. I also noticed in the distance that Miss Nearhoof had just appeared outdoors. It was her morning on duty.

Then I put my head down, shut my eyes, and allowed the noises of the playground to fill my ears.

I expected there to be an argument first, but if anything was said by either girl I didn't hear it - only a shriek as something heavy fell across my back and over onto the hard concrete.

What had I *done*? What on earth had possessed me to go along with Beryl's plan? I leapt to my feet, hoping desperately that there might still be time to save Susan from injury - or *worse*. But she lay sprawled on the concrete, frighteningly still. Beryl wasn't standing in triumph over her enemy, though. She too was on the ground, groaning and holding her stomach. Susan's foot had caught her there - hard - as she went over I found out later.

And just then Miss Nearhoof came charging towards us. As

she arrived, both girls sat up, Susan rubbing her head and inspecting her hand for blood, Beryl still clutching her stomach. Then two of Susan's admirers helped her to get up. Beryl had to manage on her own. I was standing guiltily by, unhurt but very red in the face - and all of a sudden the centre of attention, with Susan's friends now pointing at me. So it was perfectly obvious to Miss Nearhoof who must be to blame for whatever had been going on. I was the only *boy* involved.

"Do you know what I do to boys who fight with *girls*?" she bawled.

And with that she grabbed me by the bottom of my short trousers, yanked me off the ground, balanced me expertly on her trembling knee, and began slapping my exposed upper leg. It was a punishment she usually kept for boys from the nearby orphanage who had no mum or dad.

I was too mad to do anything but cry out in protest.

What I couldn't understand, though, through my ordeal, was why Susan and Beryl weren't fighting. They ought to have been going at it like cat and dog. By the time the teacher had done with me everyone else had drifted away, scared to death they might be next. But the two girls, who had both now recovered, were waiting to laugh at my shame and embarrassment. Which they did. Together.

And for a while they were the best of friends. They even appeared in our next class photograph holding hands.

5

THE YOUNG SAILOR

A tinted photograph appeared in our house one day. From nowhere - or at least that's how it seemed to me. For a time it lay flat on a shelf in the kitchen, as if my mum wasn't sure what she should do with it. Then a place was eventually found for it on the ledge of a small window on the landing. It showed a smiling young man in a sailor suit. He didn't look much like Uncle Pip, though. He had no great beard. In fact he looked too *young* to have one.

If the photograph was talked about at all, it was in whispers, but I picked up that the young man's name was Ernie. His other name was Leech, or Beech - I didn't quite hear. The picture was a bit blurred, and the colours looked faded. I thought it must be old and wasn't interested in it, in spite of the war and everything. But I did sometimes glance at it as I climbed the stairs. There were people living a few doors away who were called *Beech*, but I certainly didn't connect the picture with *them*.

Not for a moment. I hardly knew them.

But I *had* noticed them. And Mr and Mrs Beech were a bit odd I thought. They had no children, for one thing. In fact unlike most of the grown-ups on Elderberry Lane, they looked too *old* to have kids. They both had grey hair, Mr Beech's being of the silvery kind that you could see through in places. He worked for the railways, I'd heard, and always wore a black waistcoat, even when he was only pottering in the garden. What he did at the railways, I didn't know. He may have been an engine driver, though I doubted that. I thought I would be able to tell if someone had that job. He looked too old for it, and too small, somehow.

But you saw more of *Mrs* Beech. She spent a lot of time at the front window, with the curtain drawn back - watching the Yanks passing by, it seemed. Or at other times she would come outdoors for a bit and stand at the front gate, as if she was waiting anxiously for someone. She always looked *down* the lane, towards the main road and the bus stops.

Apart from Mr Beech's job, they didn't seem to have much to do to fill their lives. You rarely saw them together, even so. Mr Beech would always be at the back of the house, in the shed or garden, depending on the weather. He seemed to be busy, but there wasn't much to show for it.

The garden was partly overgrown, and nothing ever came out of the shed to explain the banging and hammering we sometimes heard. Pete never had much to say about them. He was far more interested in the big wide world beyond Elderberry Lane.

Mrs Beech started to worry me. I thought she might be a bit funny in the head. Now and then, after school at first, she'd ask me to run an errand for her. It was never for anything much, though - maybe a box of matches or a Dolly Blue, or something like that - from McMahon's shop, down on the main road. She would hurry to the front door when she saw me passing, but it was easy to guess that whatever she wanted couldn't matter very much to her. In fact it was as if she'd made it up on the spur of the moment. And when I got back from the shop she would use it as an excuse to invite me into her kitchen for a biscuit by the back door, as if I'd done her a big favour.

I didn't much like that. There was something funny about the place itself as well as Mrs Beech's head. She had a stool in the kitchen which she would sit on while she asked me a lot of questions. I felt I had to be very careful how I answered them, although there wasn't much chance of saying anything wrong because the questions were always so boring. All she wanted to know was how I was getting on at school, if I liked the teachers - that sort of thing. I did my best to answer, but the funny thing was that I could see she wasn't really listening. Not *properly.* So I would eat the biscuit as fast as I could and leave. Sometimes she would have a glass of pop ready for me, though, which took longer. We always stayed in the kitchen. The door into the front room would be closed.

I also began to notice her now and again down on the main road, standing near the bus stop. There was something queer about that, too. She wouldn't be dressed for getting on a bus. Sometimes I could see that she only had slippers on her feet, and perhaps a pinny still tied around her waist. And she never waited at the bus stop for going into town. She'd be standing close to the one across the road, instead, looking closely at the people who were getting *off* the buses - although she wouldn't be trying to speak to them. If I was near enough I could see that she often looked upset, but no one would be paying her any attention.

At first after the errands she offered me just a plain biscuit. That was until it started to happen on Saturday mornings - and even now and then on Sundays, when there would *be* no errand to run. She began to give me biscuits then that I hadn't tasted before - custard creams, and others with jam inside. Some even had bits of *chocolate* on them. She asked me which pop I liked best, and when I told her it was Dandelion & Burdock she always had a glass ready for me. It meant that I had to stay with Mrs Beech for longer.

Another change was that she was now doing most of the talking, instead of pretending to listen to me. I found it just as hard to listen to *her*, though. Her talk was all about the old days, whenever *they* were. It was a struggle not to yawn. I had to try to keep the right expression on my face, though, because I didn't want to upset her, and could see that it might easily happen. But then, through the fog, I noticed a new name. She had begun to talk about someone called *Ernest*.

I had no idea who Ernest was to begin with. I thought he might be a brother or cousin of hers - in the time long ago when she was girl. But I didn't really care, anyway. Not much. But then slowly I understood that she was talking about someone more special. Ernest had to be her own little boy, I realised.

But where was he now? The Ernest she spoke of was always just a child. She told me about taking him out in his pram, and how he learnt to walk and talk. And then gradually he grew to be old enough to go to school. Ernest was cleverer than all the other boys and girls, but he was good at other things, too. He learnt to swim and to ride a bike when he was no more than five or six, and went on to play for the school football team when he was really too young, because he was naturally so good at it. She made him sound so *brilliant* that it started to annoy me. She seemed to want to compare him with me. I could only just about stay up on a bike, and I was a long way still from being able to swim. Nor did they want me in the school football team. Not yet for a while, anyway. But I had no choice but to go on listening - with, I hoped, the right expression on my face. There was no easy escape.

She seemed to enjoy talking about Ernest - but at the same time I could see that she didn't really. She couldn't *help* it, that's how it seemed, but if her face was anything to go by she felt worse afterwards. Then one morning - it was a Sunday, so there was no errand to run - she surprised me by saying:

"What is it like to drown, do you think?"

It was the strangest question Mrs Beech had ever asked me. And I hadn't been paying enough attention. That was becoming more difficult all the time. But my mind hadn't been blank. I'd been wondering why the door into the front room was ajar for once. The door was usually firmly shut, and I had become quite curious about the front room. But I couldn't see anything through the crack.

"I don't know," I managed to say, in answer to her strange question. "I can't swim yet."

I knew at once it was a stupid answer. I meant I never went out of my depth at the baths and so was never in any danger. But she seemed not to have noticed anyway.

"Ernest was a wonderful swimmer," she said. "Just *wonderful.*" And she was off into those old days again. As she talked, I thought for the first time in my life about drowning. Once or twice when trying to swim with one foot on the bottom I had gone under. The sensation was all bubbles and pain in the nose and eyes, and *panic panic panic!* Drowning must be just like that, I thought - except that you wouldn't be able to get back to the top.

"Would you like to see some photographs of Ernest?" Mrs Beech suddenly asked.

"Yes please," I said. And I meant it. She had talked so much about him that I was keen to know what he looked like, this brilliant boy.

So she led me for the first time into her front room. The place had a funny smell, as if people only ever went in there to be unhappy. Opening a drawer, she brought out what looked like an expensive book - I'd never seen a photograph album before. We sat down on the settee to look at it, and then I lifted my eyes and saw for the first time, hanging above the mantelpiece, a coloured photograph of a young sailor. It was a bigger version of the picture we had at the top of our stairs. I went cold inside knowing in an instant that the young man had once been her little boy Ernest, and that he'd drowned somehow. Probably in the war.

Mrs Beech did her best to show me the photographs in the album, and to talk about them, but it was a struggle for her and she had to give up.

Perhaps she could tell how uncomfortable I was.

"He was a wonderful swimmer," she said again. "Very strong. And the ship wasn't very far from land when it sank, you know... But they said that no one survived. *No one at all!* Everyone went down with the ship... What would it be *like* to drown?"

I lowered my head, holding my hands together between my knees. Just for a moment, to try to make things easier, I wanted to ask her if she knew whether Ernest had ever sailed to the side of the world - that place where the sky met the sea - *before* he'd drowned, but I managed to stop myself. I thought she might soon cry, and knew I wouldn't be able to bear it... But then to my surprise she brightened.

"I think he *did* survive," she said. "No one who could swim like Ernest could *possibly* drown. Not when they were *that* close to land. He must have banged his head on something and lost his memory, that's all. One day he'll suddenly remember everything and come home, just like all the other young men. I'm *sure* of it!"

And she went across to the window, drew back the curtain, and looked expectantly down Elderberry Lane, towards the bus stops.

6
DON'T SHOOT!

It was Sunday morning again, but very early. I was lying in bed, all tense with Pete silent and still beside me. I'd been wakened for the second or third time by sharp little bangs in the distance. It was always on a Sunday.

I couldn't work out what they were.

When I first heard them, I thought the *war* might have started up again. Then I wondered if it might be one of the old cars of Elderberry Lane backfiring, but it was too early for that. Nearly everyone stayed in bed very late on Sundays. The bangs in any case were from too far off, seeming to come from the direction of some woods - the *dark* woods, as we called them - way over the fields at the back of our house. There was no pattern or rhythm to them. They could come in a rush - *crack crack crack* - followed by a long pause. Or they might be one at a time, with anywhere from a few seconds to half a minute in between, so that you held your breath as you waited for the next one.

I was sure Pete could hear them as well, but he didn't say anything. I couldn't even tell if he was properly awake. He seemed very stiff, as if he might be secretly afraid. I knew that twice recently he'd got out of bed very early, slipped into his clothes, then disappeared for a while. Luckily he got back well before anyone was up for breakfast. I was sure he'd been out investigating the bangs, but I felt scared and pretended to be asleep.

Now he seemed to prefer just to lie there.

"What *is* it?" I said at last, in a loud whisper.

His eyes had been tightly shut, but he answered instantly, without any groaning or stretching.

"The bangs? It's Tommy Fairbrother and his men."

Tommy Fairbrother was a farmer who owned most of the fields in the area - those that hadn't been swallowed up by the American base. He had two sons who'd been away in the war and had come back with wild reputations. The family wasn't much liked.

"What are they *doing*?"

"Shooting."

"You mean like when the *war* was on?"

"No, this is different."

"Shooting *what*, then?"

"Birds. Animals. *Anything*."

"Why would they do *that*?"

"I don't think they *like* them."

"But doesn't it get them into trouble?"

"With the police?" Pete laughed. "Farmers like Tommy Fairbrother can shoot just about anything they feel like. Even *people*, if they're not careful."

"*People?*"

"Yes, and not only people. *Children*, too."

This was *really* scary.

"How do you know that?"

"They tried to shoot *me*!"

It turned out that Pete had been listening to the Sunday morning bangs for longer than *I* had. And it was true that when he went missing those two Sunday mornings he'd been trying to find out about them. It hadn't taken him long to confirm that the bangs *were* coming from the woods. These were crudely fenced off with rusty wire, but he'd been able to get through and hide in the bushes. He'd seen the men firing their guns at things in the grass and up in the trees. Later he'd watched them carrying away rabbits and big, brightly coloured birds, talking and laughing while the birds were still fluttering in their hands.

Pete *hated* it, but he couldn't help being fascinated as well. In fact he was *so* fascinated that the second time he went up there he crept a bit too close. To his horror, one of the men suddenly turned and fired at *him*, without waiting to see what it *was* that was moving in the bushes. They *liked* to do that, Pete said - turn and shoot, without stopping to think. Just like the cowboys at the pictures. Luckily the shot had missed him. He then stood up with his hands held high, the way he'd seen the baddies do it in films. The men didn't even say they were sorry, though. They just shouted at him and told him to clear off if he didn't want to get himself killed.

"But haven't you told *Dad*?"

"No, he'd only shout, too. There's an old notice saying the woods are private. *And* dangerous!"

I was surprised Pete wasn't content to leave it at that, but he was still mad at the men. He wanted to get even, he said. Or at least stop Tommy Fairbrother and his gang shooting any more innocent creatures.

"What will you do?"

"I don't know yet."

A couple of Sundays later he again slipped out of bed very early and disappeared. I listened to the bangs, very worried that my brother might *really* get himself shot. Soon, mixed with the usual sort, I began to hear *louder* bangs. Did that mean the men had brought *bigger* guns?

What were they trying to shoot *now*?

At last Pete crept back into the house again and up to our room.

He got back into bed still with his clothes on, panting a bit, an excited look in his eyes.

"What *happened*?" I whispered.

"I tried to warn the animals."

"*How*?"

"I took along some old fireworks I've been keeping - bangers - and set them off just as the men were thinking of shooting."

"But didn't that tell them where you were?"

"No. I threw the bangers as far as I could, and kept on the move."

The men had been mystified to start with, but they finally spotted what was going on and chased after Pete. He could run like the wind, though, and they had their guns and stuff to carry.

I hoped desperately that he'd be satisfied now, but the very next Sunday morning he again began to climb out of bed the moment the sun came up.

"Don't go!" I pleaded, in my loudest whisper, tugging at his pyjama sleeve.

"I've *got* to."

I listened once more to the gunshots, numb with terror. This time, however, they were mixed with something *really* unexpected - the shrill sound of a policeman's whistle. Where Pete had picked *that* up I couldn't imagine. He seemed to be able to get his hands on anything he wanted. He was blowing it very loudly now, to warn the woodland creatures, and in spite of my dread I couldn't help being proud of him. It must have been harder, too, for the men to tell where this sound was coming from this time - and a policeman's whistle might well have been scaring *them*!

He told me later, though, that in the end he'd had to run for his life as usual.

"Did they kill any animals this time?" I asked him.

"I didn't wait to find out."

Pete now began to think of more ambitious ideas for thwarting Tommy Fairbrother and his murderers. He said he was going to dig a pit and cover it with branches and grass. Then they'd fall into it. He'd seen Tarzan do it in a picture, to catch a man-eating lion. I'd been with him at the time. Tarzan had fixed pointed stakes in the bottom of the pit to impale the beast. It had died making horrible cries.

"You can't do *that*!" I told him.

"Why not?"

"Tommy Fairbrother and his sons are *people*."

"I know. But think of what *they're* doing to the birds and rabbits!"

Pete crept out earlier than ever next time, carrying a spade. I was so scared I nearly wakened Dad to tell him what he was planning to do, but in the end I just waited for the worst.

He was simply *ages* coming back this time. I could tell from his face that things hadn't gone according to plan.

"They caught me digging the pit," he said.

The men had held him at gunpoint. They'd made him keep his arms raised until he could barely hold them up, all the while talking about what they would do to him if he didn't stay away from there once and for all.

"Don't shoot!" he'd pleaded, but they'd only laughed. They forced him to kneel and made him promise never to come anywhere near their woods again. - otherwise they wouldn't be responsible for their actions.

As he was running away, they even fired shots over his head.

"They're *mad*!" he said. "Those sons of his are the worst. They think they're still in the *war*. Someone's *really* going to get hurt if they carry on like that."

This didn't sound like the *real* Pete talking. He sounded defeated at last.

For a time he was completely silent about the whole business. But then to my dismay the shock *wore off*. He started to make *new* plans. And this time he wouldn't tell me what they were. I just couldn't *believe* it.

Soon he leapt out of bed and disappeared very early on Sunday morning yet again, shaking me off when I tried to stop him. I felt I really *must* tell Dad - Pete might easily get himself killed. But it seemed too late for that, somehow. So instead I got dressed myself and chased after him. I could hear that the shooting had already started.

Pete was out of sight, but I had a pretty good idea where he'd be.

There wasn't any gunfire now for some reason. Keeping low, I was getting close to the woods when I heard a single loud shot, followed instantly by a cry. I froze. Then a moment or two later he appeared from somewhere up ahead and began walking slowly in my direction. He was in a daze. I almost had to give him a shove to make him notice me.

"Pete! What's *wrong*?"

"What?"

"What's *happened*?"

"An accident."

"An *accident*? Who? What? Is anybody hurt?"

"*Killed*, I think."

I took it for granted that Pete had been involved and that it was in all likelihood his fault.

"Come on!" I said. "We'd better get home, quick!"

But he would only walk at his own slow pace.

"How did it happen, anyway?"

"One of Tommy Fairbrother's sons turned and fired, like the cowboys do. And then Tommy Fairbrother *himself* yelled out, and fell down in the grass."

"Was his son firing at *you*?"

"I couldn't tell."

"Which one *was* it?"

"I don't know. You can't tell them apart. But they're as bad as one another, so it doesn't matter."

Somehow we got back into the house without waking Mum and Dad. Then a little while afterwards, as we lay in bed, we heard what was probably a police car going by, followed soon by what could have been an ambulance. Both must have been heading up Elderberry Lane in the direction of Tommy Fairbrother's farm.

Pete got over the incident very quickly. He thought they all deserved it and said it would put an end to the shooting. But we had a tense week waiting for the police to call. It was a big relief when nobody came to arrest him. Then at the weekend Mum had the *Reporter* spread out on the kitchen table as usual, and spotted something.

"Have you seen *this*?" she said to Dad.

"Seen what?"

Pete and I were hiding just behind the door, in the front room. We hardly dared breathe. We knew what it was going to be about.

"Tommy Fairbrother's been shot - by one of those *sons* of his, they think."

"*Murdered*, d'you mean? Can't say I'm surprised."

"No, just shot in the shoulder."

"Isn't he dead, then?"

"No. More's the pity."

"It *was* on purpose, though?"

"It says not. Just an accident. They were out killing rabbits."

There was a silence, and then I really had to admire Pete's nerve.

"Was anybody else involved?" he asked, strolling casually into the kitchen.

Mum gave him a funny look, but said not according to the report in the paper.

7
THE LEECHES

You would think our Pete loved *all* the creatures under the dome of the blue-glass sky, but that wasn't *quite* true. There were the leeches in the pit.

"They fasten onto passing fish with their mouths and suck the blood out of them," he told me, on another morning when we were still in bed. He did a lot of his thinking then. And talking.

"Why do they do that?" I asked.

"It's how they *live.*"

"On *blood*? That isn't food!"

"It is to them. I think they *could* find other food to eat if they wanted to, but that wouldn't be any fun for them, would it?"

"It doesn't *sound* like fun."

"They *love* it. That's why they'll never let go - not until the poor fish is completely empty. They have these horrible mouths, and once they start to suck the blood out, that's it. You wouldn't be able to pull the leech off the fish even with a pair of pliers. They only let go when *they* decide."

"How long does it take them?"

"That's up to them. They can make it last all day if they want to. Or even longer. It all depends how much they're enjoying it. Just think of the poor fish, swimming innocently through the water, minding its own business - and then *that* happens!"

"But can't we *stop* them?"

"How?"

"We should be able to think of *something*."

I expected Pete to be bursting with ideas and keen to dash to the pit the minute he'd jumped into his clothes. As often happened, though, he suddenly lost interest. He started going on instead about something called the Olympic Games. The next Olympics were going to be held in London, he told me. I was only half listening, though. I couldn't get the leeches out of my mind so easily.

As soon as we were up and I was able to escape from the house, I dashed round to tell Johnny Stone about them. For once he didn't make an argument.

"We've got to *stop* them," he said, hardly able to keep still.

"But how can we do it?"

"*Catch* them. That's the only way. Let's find some others, and get nets and jam jars and stuff."

"What will we do with the leeches after we've *caught* them."

"We'll decide that later. Come on!"

It was the middle of the school holidays again and the sun was shining, as it usually did, but not many families were away. Day trips by charabanc were al that could be afforded. So we knew we weren't going to have much trouble rounding up a gang. We found a couple of seaside fishing nets and an empty jar in Johnny's shed, and set off.

Keith Foster and his weedy brother Barry were sitting on the low wall at the front of their house, kicking their heels.

"We're all going to the pit," we shouted. "Come on!"

"The pit? Why? Has somebody *drowned*?"

"No, it's the *leeches*. They're killing the fish. We've got to *stop* them. Have you got any old jam jars or fishing nets?"

"What for?"

"To *catch* them."

"Oh."

They didn't wait to be told more, but jumped up and ran indoors. A few seconds later they were back, carrying a net each, and started to run with us.

Just then we saw one of the Quarry brothers - their Dennis - coming up the lane. He was only our age, so there shouldn't be any trouble when he was on his own. But we kept moving anyway.

"What's *happening*?" he said, picking up our excitement.

"It's the *leeches*."

"What leeches? Where?"

"In the pit. We're going to *kill* them."

"Why?"

"They're sucking all the blood out of the fish. Right this very minute. We've got no time to lose. Have you got any old jam jars?"

"At home, yeah. I'll be back in a minute!"

And he dashed off up to their house.

We didn't wait for Dennis Quarry, but broke into a trot again. Next we waved to Jimmy Whittam, who was in his front window gazing out at the world. He came rushing to the door.

"What's going on?"

"It's the *leeches*. They're killing the fish in the pit. Come on! We're going to give them a taste of their own medicine. Bring a fishing net, or any old jam jars you can find!"

"OK. I'll look in the shed."

Soon Jimmy was catching us up, carrying *three* nets - with Dennis Quarry close behind, a jam jar in each hand. I'd never known one of the Quarrys join in anything before. They normally stuck to bullying.

But the boy we really didn't want with us was little Malcolm Bailey, who never seemed to grow any bigger. He was always hanging around, his nose usually snotty. His mum and dad didn't seem to care what he got up to. We'd heard his dad had been in prison. Now he was standing right in our path, hoping to join the adventure.

"Get lost!" we snarled, shoving him out of the way without breaking stride. He wasn't so easy to get rid of, though, and started following at a distance.

The pit was a natural pond in the middle of the back field - *Kelly's* field.

We'd been told many times that the pit was bottomless, but that hadn't kept us away, although we hadn't forgotten. But the only creatures living in it were the little fish we called *jackies*, along with a few frogs and newts at certain times of year. That at any rate was what we'd believed till now.

The pit was mostly covered with green stuff, which closed up again if you tried to part it with your hand. *Ginny Greenteeth*, the grown-ups called it.

If ever you fell in the stuff would drag you under, they warned us. It could even reach out as you walked past and *pull* you in. You wouldn't have a chance then, they said.

The back field was the only one in our neighbourhood that wasn't owned by Tommy Fairbrother but by another farmer - Kelly, as we called him. His farm was miles away up the main road somewhere. He was a big man, who looked like Desperate Dan from a distance. He seemed to have a moustache, or even a beard, though none of us had ever seen his face close up. As with Tommy Fairbrother and his sons, when Kelly came into view it was time to run for your life. We weren't so frightened of him, though - he was somehow too slow and clumsy to catch anyone. But like any farmer, he did his best to keep trespassers off his land - especially kids. We thought he had spies on Elderberry Lane.

There was a path running alongside the field, then you had to duck under a barbed-wire fence and cross open ground to get to the pit. That was when it would be easiest for the spies to spot you. When we reached it, though, there would be plenty of bushes to keep us out of sight.

"We'll use the cows," said Johnny, who often tried to take charge when there was no one older around. There was nobody to hear us, but he spoke in a loud whisper. Like most years, Kelly had cattle grazing in his field.

"Cows?" someone said. "For what?"

"For *cover*," our leader explained, as if it should be obvious. "Let's get moving!"

Like Indian braves expertly keeping themselves concealed in desert land, we slipped from cow to cow. Only little Malcolm Bailey, who didn't get what we were doing, could have been giving the game away. He was still dogging our footsteps, even though we kept hissing at him to push off.

Some of the cows were close to the water, chewing the cud. They shook their heads at us and tried to give us scary looks with their big brown eyes. But we knew that didn't mean a thing and took no notice of them as we gazed out over the green expanse.

"OK, has everybody got a net and a jar?" Johnny asked, in a louder voice that wasn't easy to ignore. "Good - so let's get to work! Everyone spread out around the edge!"

I was surprised that Dennis Quarry was willing to put up with Johnny's bossiness. By this point I'd expected him to be pushing weedy Barry Foster around, causing a fight with Keith, or making some other trouble. Today, though, we had serious business to attend to and he seemed happy just to be one of the gang.

Soon we were in position and stretching to dip our nets as far out in the green stuff as we could. It was very hard work - trying not to fall in at the same time.

"Got any yet?" everyone was soon asking.

"Only jackies so far."

"Plenty of green stuff in my net."

"What do leeches look like, anyway?"

"Sort of like black worms."

"Can't see anything like that."

"My arms are really aching."

"So are mine."

And that's the way it went on, until our arms were aching so much we could hardly hold the nets.

"This is no good," somebody said at last. It was the general feeling.

We looked at Johnny.

"Just think of what they're *doing*!" he shouted. "Think of the poor fish dying slowly like that! Having the *blood* sucked out of them!"

It kept us going for a little longer, but we still had no leeches in our nets. And by now even Johnny was growing tired. He was frowning, too as if he was trying to think of a new plan. But there was no time for that... because at that very moment we heard a sudden cry, followed by a loud splash.

One of the angrier cows was standing triumphantly at the water's edge, and *in* the water was little Malcolm Bailey. It *had* to be him. No one else was missing. We couldn't *see* him, though - only a ragged hole in the green stuff where he'd fallen through, which even as we watched was quickly filling up again.

Nobody could move. The world stood still for an endless moment. Then at last his head appeared and he slowly stood up. He seemed only to have slipped under. So the pit wasn't *bottomless*, after all! The water was *shallow*! It barely reached his short trousers, small as he was.

Shooing the cow away, we pulled him up onto the bank before his feet could begin to sink into the muddy bottom. He was coughing and crying and dripping wet, with bits of green stuff stuck to his skin, hair and and clothes - but *safe*. We told him he'd soon dry off in the sun, and not to be a baby.

"Look at his *legs*, though!" someone shouted.

We all looked. And stuck to them were loads of black, worm-like things.

"*Leeches*!"

Little Malcolm Bailey saw the things himself, and screamed. He'd heard what we'd said about them sucking the blood out of fish and was expecting the same thing to happen to *him*.

"Shut up while we get them off!" ordered Johnny. "Someone fetch a stick and jar!"

Little Malcolm Bailey struggled to remove the leeches himself, but two of us held his arms until we could flick them safely into a jar of pond water. We were surprised when they came off quite easily. And now the horrible things were our prisoners - we could do as we *liked* with them. It was a delicious feeling. Everybody agreed that they deserved the worst punishment we could possibly dream up. We were already begining to think about what we would do to them as, too impatient now to bother with cover, we made our way back to the path. Little Malcolm Bailey was wailing behind while still checking for more leeches on his legs. He looked in a terrible mess, wet through to the skin, but it was only the noise he was making that bothered us.

Then someone yelled, "*Kelly*!"

As always, the big farmer was in the distance. He'd probably been tipped off. We felt certain he must have seen us. Taking care we didn't spill the contents of the jar, we ducked down into long grass, pulling little Malcolm Bailey down with us. Then a hand was clamped over his mouth to shut the stupid boy up. We saw Kelly inspect his field from one corner, shielding his eyes from the sun. Then he lifted his hat, scratched his head, and started to wander off. He really was hopeless. For a moment we felt like shouting and waving to him.

The rest of the way home we talked gleefully about how best to put the horrible leeches to death. Everyone had an idea.

"Let's drop them in boiling water," suggested Jimmy Whittam. "Or better still, put them in cold water and then *boil* it."

"That's too *tame*," said Dennis Quarry, still surprisingly very much one of the team. "Let's make a fire and roast them alive. But *slowly*."

"We could drop them from a bedroom window onto the concrete, and then *stamp* on them," thought weedy Barry Foster.

No one believed that idea was any good at all. The leeches would barely feel it.

"I know how to make it *really* bad for them," said Johnny, with more authority. "Let's roast them for a bit, then make cuts in them with a razor blade. And after that we can pour vinegar over them. Vinegar's an *acid* so it's sure to sting a lot."

Johnny's mum and dad were both out, so his house was the one we could go to without being disturbed. Nothing needed to be said, but we all knew that we didn't want anyone older to see what we were getting up to. Little Malcolm Bailey was still with us, but beginning at last to get the message. We closed the front gate to keep him out, too excited by the thought of what we had in store for the leeches to think of taking him home to explain what had happened. But his mum wouldn't have been much bothered, anyway. She was a funny woman.

"See that sawn-off tree stump down at the bottom of the garden," said Johnny, when we reached the back of the house. "We can use it as sort of a table. I'll get the stuff." It was his house, so no one was going to argue about doing it his way. "Find some dry twigs to make a fire."

He disappeared indoors for a while, then came out with a box of matches, one of his dad's old razor blades, a fork, and a vinegar bottle.

Leaving room on the tree stump for the later cutting and soaking-in-acid stages, we arranged the twigs we'd gathered into a little bonfire. While we were striking matches and blowing on the fire to get it going, Johnny fished one of the bigger leeches out of the jar with the fork. We had it wriggling on the tree stump, completely at out mercy - when there was a sudden commotion behind. I swung around and was surprised to see that it was *Pete*.

"Just what are you lot doing?" he shouted angrily. "I saw you all at the pit."

No one could explain. The evidence was right there in front of us. For a moment it looked as if he was going to give us all a good thumping.

But instead he grabbed the jar off Johnny and using a stray twig carefully dropped the leech back into it to rejoin its friends.

He held the jar up to his face to make sure they were all OK, then stormed off without another word. From Johnny's garden fence we soon spotted him on the path in the distance, almost running back to the pit with them.

I was completely baffled, but too scared to challenge Pete later about what had happened and why he'd done what he had. He said nothing himself. His mind, I could see, had moved onto other things as ever. The Olympic Games, most likely. The leeches aside, he seemed to be thinking of little else lately - especially a man called Jessie somebody. I waited for a better moment - in bed next morning.

"Why did you save the leeches we caught?" I demanded to know, while he was still sleepy.

"What?" he said, rubbing his eyes.

"The leeches, from the pit. Yesterday - you know."

"Leeches?" It was almost as if he'd forgotten all about them.

"From the pit."

"I don't know anything about leeches.""

"Yes you do. Why did you save them?"

"*Save* them? ... Oh yeah - what about it?"

"You said you *hated* the things."

Pete yawned - a great big yawn.

"I *do*."

"So why *save* them, then?"

"Just because we hate them, it doesn't give us the right to *kill* them does it?"

"Why not? Look at what *they* do to the poor fish! That's what *you* said."

"I know they're cruel, but it's their *nature*."

"Nature? What's that? Why does that matter?"

He yawned again. "They can't *help* what they do."

"But doesn't it make you hate them?"

"Yes, I've already said that."

"So it's all right for us to kill them, then? They *deserve* it."

"No they don't."

"Why not?"

"They just *don't*, that's all... Hey, there was this great athlete, a black man named Jesse Owens who won four gold medals in the last Olympics, before the war. *Four gold medals*! Just think of *that*!"

8

AUNTIE KATE

I had two favourite aunties, though I never talked about that to anyone.

It was a kind of secret. There was my Auntie Jessie, the one who saved my life after we'd painted Billy Stringer's dad's car, but she lived a troubled life a bus ride away in a rough part of town and we didn't see her very often. I liked her a lot, even so, but my *special* favourite was my Auntie Kate, my mum's youngest sister. She lived much closer - just across the main road, in fact, near the bus stops. She was married to Uncle Pip. He drove a lorry now, carting loads of sand about. He'd shaved off the great beard he'd had when he was a sailor in the war. She was really beautiful, Auntie Kate, with long dark hair and a pretty smile. She even wore lipstick, something my mum would never do.

Well, one afternoon this favourite auntie of mine came to meet me from school for some reason. It was only a short walk and no trouble for her, but I certainly didn't *need* to be met and was embarrassed. I was too big now. I found that part of me didn't really mind, though, and I was half glad when she started to make a bit of a habit of it. I liked the others to notice Auntie Kate. And they did. Even Susan Granger.

I was still as potty as ever about Susan, and as far away, too, from being able to talk to her. I couldn't manage to get out a single word. But worse than that, if I was within *ten yards* of her my cheeks would begin to go red. *And* my ears. It didn't happen to anyone else I knew, but I could feel them burning. Susan never even glanced at me, though, whether my face was red or not, so I was pleased to notice that she couldn't help looking at my Auntie Kate, smiling as she waited to meet me at the school gate. Sometimes Auntie Kate would give me a hug. This ought to have given me the creeps, but with her I didn't mind at all. It was almost as if I had a real girlfriend, and what's more one who was even prettier than Susan.

It didn't last for very long, though. Maybe Auntie Kate understood at last that I was really far too big now to have someone meet me from school. But she still came over to our house a lot and was often there when I got home. She and my mum would be talking about something very boring over a cup of tea, but I liked to hang around them all the same. Auntie Kate was good to *be* near, somehow.

But then I began to notice another change. It worried me. Auntie Kate had always had what my mum called a good figure, but now she seemed to be growing fat. Her stomach was getting to be very big. You could tell even if she had a coat on. I was so worried about it that I asked Pete if he knew what was wrong with her. He frowned. He'd noticed the change, too.

"I think she's got a *baby* inside her," he said. "I can't think of anything else."

"A *baby*?"

"Yeah."

"*Inside* her?"

"That's right."

"But how did it *happen*?"

"Uncle Pip must have done it."

"You mean he *put* it in there."

"Sort of, yeah."

"But *how?*"

Pete hesitated, then he started to describe something weird and amazing and sort of exciting. I stopped asking questions. I knew he'd been trying to tell me about all this for ages, but now for the first time I really wanted to hear - now that it involved Auntie Kate. But something else had always held him back. It had been as if Pete himself couldn't quite believe it. He seemed a little more sure of himself now, though, and as he was talking - trying to explain at last - I began to understand what the problem had been. Besides being weird and amazing and all the rest of it, it also sounded *horrible*.

"Not Uncle Pip!" I said, when he got to the end at last. "He wouldn't do *that* to her!! She wouldn't *let* him!"

But Pete insisted that there was no other way of getting a baby into a woman.

I couldn't face Auntie Kate for a while after that and stayed out of her way. But she was still growing fatter, and I got so anxious about it that I was almost able to forget what she and Uncle Pip had been getting up to when they should have been asleep in bed. The important thing was, what was going to *happen* to her? How was the baby ever going to get *out?* I lay awake at night, worrying about it. And for once Pete was no help. He was worried, too. It looked impossible, he had to admit. Poor Auntie Kate!

She disappeared into hospital one day, though, and a few weeks later was pushing a baby around in a pram, a little boy called Jack. I couldn't understand where he'd got his *name* from, but nobody seemed interested in that. They just wanted to look in the pram and smile at him making funny baby noises. I felt unhappy about the whole thing. I'd lost Auntie Kate, it seemed. She had no interest in *me* now, and she certainly never came to meet me from school any more after Baby Jack arrived. She just wanted to show off her new baby to everyone.

One thing I was discovering at school now was that I was very good at drawing. Not *painting*. I couldn't stay inside the lines when I did that. It didn't seem important to me. But drawing with a pencil was different. I did it at home, too. I didn't know where I'd got the idea from - it didn't interest Pete - but I started to spend a lot of time at it. My mum worked in a pub most evenings, and I would try to do a drawing to leave for her when she got home. That would be very late, so I was always asleep in bed by then. I never copied things, but somehow I knew how to make a drawing of a dog look like a dog, or a boat like a boat. It was easy for me. And my mum never forgot to say something next morning about whatever it was I'd left for her, even though she herself couldn't draw for toffee.

It made me want to draw for others, too, but that wasn't so easy. I mean it was hard to get anyone else to notice what I'd done. They might glance at a drawing for a moment, but that was all. Even our nice new teacher, Mrs Ford, rarely made a comment. Most of the time she wanted us to paint squares, like a draughts board, taking the utmost care never to go outside the lines. The others in the class soon learnt that that was the easiest way to win praise from her, and needless to say, Susan Granger's squares were the best of all. Even if I managed to do it neatly, the colours would always end up running.

After my mum, the next person I thought of drawing something for at home was my Auntie Kate. She wasn't coming to our house quite so often any more, though. I left my drawings lying about when I knew she was likely to visit, but since I was usually at school I could never be sure she'd seen them. I thought of trying to make them especially good for her, to catch her attention, but I did that with every drawing anyway. I didn't want to put Auntie Kate's name on them because I was worried that it might upset Mum. She seemed to think every drawing I did was for *her*.

Then I thought of drawing babies - if only I could. I didn't have the patience to do a lot of studying, but you had to have an *idea* of what something looked like before you could draw it. The trouble with babies was that they were always wrapped up in shawls, with even their heads covered. Or they were lost in a pram. Until he got to the crawling stage my efforts at drawing Baby Jack weren't going to be very good. But in any case I knew it would always be very difficult for me to compete with the attractions of a *real* baby.

By the time I'd waited for Baby Jack to become more visible the idea of doing drawings of him for Auntie Kate had begun to seem pointless. It had needed to be when he was a little baby, somehow - when he was still *new*. But I was seeing much less of her now, in any case. She and Uncle Pip lived with my grandma and grandad, in their small terraced house down on the main road, but now that they had a baby they were looking for a house of their own. They might soon disappear from our lives altogether, I was realising. Not that I cared desperately about that. My own life had moved on a bit, too.

Then something happened that brought Auntie Kate right back into my thoughts and worries. One dark morning, before school, a boy called Ronnie Kirwin who lived next door to them came tearing over to our house for my mum. it wasn't very far, but he was out of breath.

"It's Auntie Kate," he gasped. "She isn't well. Grandma said come quick!"

I went to school feeling only a little bit anxious. I knew people were often ill. I myself had had German measles and chicken pox, and Pete had had the mumps, too. I thought Auntie Kate must have something like that, in which case she was sure to be better soon. But when I got home I could tell at once that this was something more serious. Auntie Kate had been taken into hospital in an ambulance, I picked up. Mum was staying off work, which was *very* unusual.

I asked what was wrong. Children were never told much - you had to *listen* if you wanted to find something out. But this was different.

"She's had a haemorrhage," Mum said. She wasn't looking at me. It was almost as though she was talking to herself.

"What's that?"

"Bleeding. She's lost a lot of blood."

"She's *cut* herself, you mean?"

"No, not that."

"Why did she bleed, then?"

"It was to do with the baby."

"You mean Baby Jack's been bleeding, too?"

"No, Baby Jack's all right. It's only Auntie Kate who was bleeding. It was where the baby came from."

"Oh." I didn't know what else to say for a moment. My mind filled with horrible pictures of what might have happened.

"Will she be all right?" I asked at last.

"We don't know. She's got to have a blood transfusion."

"What's that?"

"They put someone else's blood into you."

"To fill you up?"

"Sort of. But they can go wrong."

"How?"

"It's when they use the wrong sort of blood, or something."

"But they wouldn't do *that*, would they?"

"It sometimes doesn't match properly, the doctors say."

"That won't happen to Auntie Kate, though, will it?"

"We don't know yet. We've got to wait."

The waiting lasted for three days and nights. On the third night a car arrived at our house, long after bedtime. I didn't see it, I only heard it draw up outside, followed by the sound of voices. Then I heard our front door being quietly closed.

I couldn't manage to get to sleep again for a long time after that. Then it was morning all of a sudden and my dad was giving me a gentle shake to waken me. Pete was already awake.

"I'm sorry, you won't be seeing your Auntie Kate again," Dad told me, in a hushed voice.

I could see that Pete had been crying a bit. I watched him getting silently into his clothes, his eyes looking at nothing at all. Then I climbed out of bed myself, surprised somehow that I was able to do it. It was as if I wasn't really there - like I was in a film, or something. Or like the feeling you got of being in another world, separated from everyone else, when you went under at the swimming baths.

There was talk of us staying off school, but in the end we went in late. Dad wrote a note for both of us to explain what had happened. Mrs Ford spoke to the class in a quiet, serious voice. Nobody looked at me, but I could tell I was the centre of attention, all the same. Later a few of them asked if it was the auntie who used to meet me after school, the pretty one, who'd died. They didn't crowd around me but approached me separately. With a sad expression on my face, I told them yes. I was secretly enjoying feeling important. I still hadn't come close to crying.

Not so my mum. She cried all the time, especially on the day of the funeral. Only the men went. My grandfather believed women shouldn't be allowed at funerals because of all the crying they did. I was puzzled because I'd seen already Uncle Pip crying once, without caring *who* was watching.

Mum was soon going to work again, upset as she was. I still wanted to do a drawing for her each night as well, but I didn't know what to draw now. Then I thought of something that might help her to stop crying so much. I had a go at drawing Auntie Kate. I tried my best to make it look as much like her as possible and was very pleased with the result. But to my surprise Mum didn't talk about the drawing next morning. Not at first.

Later she asked me not to do any more, without saying why.

Soon after that Mrs Ford took us on a school bus outing to a farm. She'd told us to bring sketch pads along, and after we'd had a look at a few pigs and chickens and mooched around in the barns she suggested we find a place to sit quietly and draw something. I found a spot on some grass and began to draw the farmhouse and some other buildings, doing my very best as usual.

I got so absorbed that I didn't notice someone creep up behind me. Then I heard a voice - a *girl's* voice. I looked around and saw that Susan Granger was standing there quietly watching me.

"That's very *good*," she said.

I tried my hardest to say something in reply, but I could tell that my ears were already beginning to burn. The most I could do was sort of nod politely. She didn't linger.

9
PETE'S OLYMPICS

Kelly's field backed right onto the houses on our side of the bottom end of Elderberry Lane. Sometimes he planted crops there, but more often there were cows in the field, as when we went fishing for leeches. They liked to munch the privet hedge at the bottom of our garden, though usually they were content with eating the grass, keeping it short. This made the field very tempting for playing football or other games, if you could ignore the cowpats. Sometimes we almost got away with it, but Kelly's spies would sooner or later make sure that our game was spoiled. We still tried to use it, even so. There was really nowhere else.

The best view of the field was from our bedroom window. After Auntie Kate died I liked to sit up there on the window ledge, with the curtains drawn behind me. I watched the cows, sometimes sketching them if they came near enough. I thought, too, in those quiet moments, about the flat world we lived on, which I knew was also round. Kelly's field itelf was flat, like all the farmland surrounding Elderberry Lane, so that on a really clear day, with no hills blocking the view, you sometimes felt you could almost see the place, in the far, far distance, long after the land ended, where the sea lapped up against the sky… But I found I could never think about *that* for very long, and thinking in any case wasn't the idea. Sitting there behind the curtains, just looking out at the field, made me feel better somehow. I don't know why. It didn't matter that there wouldn't be much going on.

Late one afternoon, though, I was surprised to see our *Pete* down there.

Besides thinking *his* own thoughts, Pete liked to try things out on his own. He never told me what he was up to if he was busy with something new. I had to work it out for myself. So now I began to watch him quietly, trying to guess.

It wasn't too difficult this time. I could see that he was practicing a jump of some kind. But I only knew about people jumping as *high* as they could, over a bar of some sort. Pete didn't have a bar. He had marked a line in the ground with the heel of his shoe, and now he was running up to it at top speed and jumping as *far* as he could. Height didn't seem to matter. After landing he put something on the grass to mark the position, then he measured how far he'd jumped by counting the few strides it took him to get back to the line. So far so easy. But then he turned and started striding in the other direction, going way beyond the place where he'd just landed - maybe four or five times as far.

"It's *impossible!*" he said to me later.

"Impossible? What is?"

"Jumping *that* far."

"*How* far?"

"More than twenty-six feet. That's nearly *nine yards*. I've measured it out."

"But why are you trying to jump *that* far?"

"Because that's the distance *Jesse Owens* jumped in the Olympics, before the war. It's called the *long* jump. He got one of his gold medals for it."

Pete had picked up a magazine about the Olympics Games - off one of the Yanks at the base, most likely. It had pictures of Jesse Owens, some coloured, and also of Hitler, the German leader, who was now dead. The next Games would be taking place in London, Pete had been telling me, but the *last* Olympics had been held in Berlin, the capital of Germany.

"Jesse Owens was the big star," he said. "Hitler was desperate for him not to win any gold medals because he was black, but he won *four*.

He beat all the best Germans."

With the war being so recent, it was hard not to feel pleased about that, even if you'd never seen a black man.

"I want to try out the other events Jesse Owens did," Pete said. "But I'll need your help."

"On the back field? OK."

We tried the hundred metres. That had taken the great athlete only about ten seconds.

"A metre is like a long yard," Pete explained. So we paced out a hundred of them, stretching our legs as far as we could. Then my job was to count while Pete ran the distance.

"Count slowly!" he said. "That's what *real* seconds are like."

It still took him about seventeen, even so. After that we paced out *two*-hundred metres. That distance had taken Jesse Owens no more than twenty-two seconds. I took care to count even more slowly than for the first event, but Pete's time was way past thirty. His fourth medal had been won in a relay race, Pete told me, with three other runners. So there was no way of making a proper comparison. The relay gold medal had upset

Hitler just as much, though, I was glad to hear.

Pete himself wasn't upset. Trying out the different events had only increased his admiration for Jesse Owens. And he was more anxious than ever for the London Games to begin.

"Will Jesse Owens be racing this time?" I asked him.

"No," he said bitterly. "They say he's too old now. It just isn't *fair*. It's twelve years since the Olympics were held in Germany. They're supposed to be every *four* years, but they had to be cancelled when the war was on. If the war had never happened, Jesse Owens could have won easily again."

The way Pete talked about the coming Olympic Games, you would have thought he had some chance of *seeing* them. But we lived a very long way from London. Also, no one else I knew had heard of them yet. Very few other kids listened to the wireless or looked at the paper the way *he* did. So it was mostly just in Pete's head.

We might have hoped for something in the newsreel at the pictures, even so. It gave us a more interesting glimpse of what was happening in the world than the wireless or papers. But the glimpse could be very brief.

There would be a main feature and B-picture to be fitted into the cinema programme, along with a cartoon most weeks and the trailers for coming attractions. And then when the newsreel finally came on we would have to sit through a bit about politics, or what the king and queen had been up to, followed by a beauty contest, maybe, or an item involving chimps that was supposed to be funny. Only after that would the newsreel give us what we *really* wanted - the latest from the world of sport. That would normally be only football or cricket, though. It was beginning to look as if the Olympic Games might be over before we got to see or hear anything about them.

So when Pete started trying to persuade some of the older boys in the neighbourhood to have our own Olympic Games on Kelly's field, they just weren't interested. They hadn't heard of putting the shot or throwing the discus, javelin or hammer, and certainly not of the pole vault or hop step and jump. It was as if he was making it up. He tried explaining how the Games had started long ago in ancient Greece, and showed them the magazine with the colour pictures of his great hero Jesse Owens, but that made no difference, either - especially when he had to confess that Jesse Owens was now too *old* to race.

"How old *is* he?" one of these older boys asked.

Pete hesitated. "Oh… about thirty now."

"*That* old!"

"But he was still the greatest athlete of all time!" he said indignantly.

"Faster than anyone racing today. Don't ever forget that*!*"

"What's an athlete, anyway?"

"A runner. That's what they mainly do in the Olympics. *Race.* Lots of different distances… We could even have our own *marathon.*"

"Our what?"

"It's a very long race - more than twenty-six miles. That's exactly the distance a messenger once had to run - long ago in ancient Greece. He was bringing the people some very important news."

"What sort of news?"

"Something about a battle, I expect. But that isn't important. What is important is the *tradition.*" I wondered if Pete had got that word out of the magazine as well.

"Why does that matter?" the questioner said.

"Well, because everyone *thinks* it does."

"And did this Jesse Owens run those races, then - marathons? When he was still young enough."

"No, he was a *sprinter...*"

And so it went on. Pete just wasn't getting anywhere. It all sounded interesting enough to me, but the older boys were only laughing at him. It was no good. His dream of holding our very own Olympic Games on the back field soon had to be abandoned. It forced him to do a lot of new thinking - mostly each morning as he lay in bed...

And then to my surprise he came up with an answer.

"You know what?" he said. "I'm going to do it all myself... You can be my assistant and coach."

"All what?"

"All the running and jumping and throwing."

"What's a coach?"

"A *trainer.*"

"Oh." I knew it couldn't be a kind of bus.

So we made a long list of all the different races and jumps and throwing events. A *programme*, he called it. The various distances could easily be measured out by striding again. All except the marathon, that was. For that Pete worked out that he would have to run around the edge of the field *ninety-six* times. But he was going to leave that till the end.

"The marathon is always held on the last day of the Games," he told me. "It's the tradition."

Well, most of the events in the programme didn't take very long to complete, the shorter races especially. The throwing events were more awkward. Pete couldn't find anything better than an old house brick for putting the shot, and for the javelin a garden cane weighted at one end. The discus was even more of a problem. He had to use an old plate - or several. When he threw them they kept breaking. The pole vault and the high jump were over a string tied to two canes stuck in the ground. The pole he used was the old handle of a sweeping brush he'd found in our shed. It didn't help much. In fact the height he cleared was *less* than for the straightforward jump.

But nothing would put him off. He kept at it, doing a bit more each day after school, and sometimes at weekends. We carefully noted down his times and heights and distances, until we had what looked like quite an impressive official record of his results. And at last the day came when he had only the marathon left to run.

"I'm going to do that in stages, over the weekend," he announced.

"Twelve stages of eight laps."

It sounded a lot, especially as by now Pete looked worn out.

To measure the longer times the best we had was an alarm

clock.

I would count the laps and try to measure the time for each lap. He was more determined than ever - but after a mere three laps of the first stage he could barely stand up.

"Come on!" I shouted into his ear. "You can do it!" It was what he'd told me a coach should say.

But he could hardly keep moving forward...

Then I glanced across to the corner where the cows usually came back into the field after milking - something we had to do the whole time when we were playing on the field.

"*Kelly*!" I shouted.

"Where?"

But Pete was too exhausted to make a run for it.

As the big farmer came towards us I got to see him up close for the first time. He looked pretty scary, with a red face under the brim of his hat a straggly beard and moustache, and black flashing eyes like Long John Silver's. Poor Pete hadn't a hope of escaping. There was nothing I could do to help him - I had my *own* life to save. As I looked back from a safe distance, I saw that Kelly had him by the collar and was trying to march him off the field, with Pete stumbling and falling. It looked bad.

I wasn't expecting to see my brother again for a long time - if ever.

So I was *flabbergasted* when he came home after no more than an hour, looking quite fresh.

"What *happened*?" I cried, almost expecting to hear that Kelly and his men had tortured him.

"Nothing much," he said with a grin. "His wife made me a nice cup of tea and gave me a slice of homemade cake. They were very kind."

"*Kind?*"

"Well, *he* wasn't at first. Not when he was shoving me into his old car. I didn't know what to expect at the farm, though I was sure he'd send for the police. But then his *wife* came in, and she was much nicer. She said I looked tired out. So I told them about the Olympics, and what I'd been doing when he'd caught me. They seemed to know nothing about it. I explained all about Jesse Owens and the way he'd upset Hitler, and the ancient Greeks and the marathon, and the Games in London and a lot of other stuff besides, and soon Kelly himself seemed nicer, too. He even started *smiling*. They were very pleased about it all, somehow. I don't know why. It was then, anyway, that Kelly's wife put the kettle on and brought in the cake she'd made. It was as if she'd made it specially for *me*. And afterwards he even gave me a lift home."

"But weren't you *scared* all the time?"

"No, they're friendly people when you get to know them. A lot nicer than Tommy Fairbrother and his sons, that's for sure!"

When we tried showing the record we'd made of his achievements to the older boys we'd talked to, though, they were still far from impressed. On the front he'd written:

PETE'S OLYMPICS
IN HONOUR OF JESSE OWENS
GREATEST ATHLETE OF ALL TIME!

But it made no difference.

"Do you mean to say you raced against *yourself?*" one of them said.

"How *stupid!*"

I glanced at Pete - and for once he didn't have an answer. *I* wasn't really sure why he'd done it, and it looked as if he was starting to wonder himself.

It did seem a bit screwy.

After that I could tell he was losing interest in the Olympics at last. He no longer talked about them all the time, and wasn't looking in the paper or listening to the wireless for news of the London Games any more. Then in the newsreel at the pictures one Saturday afternoon, after film of just a few of the events, we were sad to see that the closing ceremony had already happened. The Games had passed us by. Now we would have to wait for the *next* Olympics - in Helsinki, Finland, in four years time, the newsreel report said. That's if we were still interested. There was *no* chance that Jesse Owens would be running *there*.

But then I heard that a full-length colour film had been made of the whole London Games. And everybody saw *that* when it came out, and talked of nothing else for ages. Everybody saw it, that is, except our Pete. He missed it. In fact he refused to go.

I was full of it myself when I got home from the pictures.

"Harrison Dillard won the hundred metres," I told him excitedly. "He ran very nearly as fast as *Jesse Owens* did. He was a black man as well. An American. The athletes were from all over the world, though. There was this blonde woman from Holland, *Fanny Blankers* something. She won all the women's races. But the *big* star was this long-distance runner with a funny foreign name again. *Emil Zatopek*. An English runner did come second in the marathon, though. You should've seen how *shattered* they all were at the end. I'm going to do some drawings…"

I could have talked all night about it, but I could see that Pete had stopped listening by now. His mind had moved on to other things again.

10
POOR MARY

Johnny Stone went to the other school. There were two, so there was a choice. Why Johnny and I were sent to different schools I never found out. No one else in Elderberry Lane went to the other school except Mary Bailey, little Malcolm's Bailey's big sister. Johnny never walked to school with Mary, though. Boys just didn't walk with girls - or *couldn't*. Girls were too different, somehow.

But *no one* bothered much with Mary, even though she was quite a pretty girl. She didn't seem to have any friends. In fact you didn't *see* her very often. She wasn't allowed out much, while her little brother hardly ever seemed to be allowed *in*. They were an odd family. The mother and father never spoke to one another, people said. Sometimes they might be on the same bus, but they would sit in separate seats, well apart. Then they would walk home up Elderberry Lane separately. She used the front door. He always went in by the back.

Mr Bailey never talked to anyone else, either. He used to make a strange *noise* sometimes - something between a bark and a shout – but that was all. He wasn't trying to speak or catch someone's attention. He didn't seem able to help it. But nor did he ever look embarrassed or say he was sorry. He just continued on his way, all alone. He was a tall, thin man with plastered-down hair that was turning grey, and a wet-looking sharp red nose.

Mrs Bailey also didn't get on with people, but for different reasons. She shouted all the time, always in a pinny, with her hair under a scarf and a cigarette stuck in her mouth. Outdoors or in, it was just the same. You could hear her through the walls. It could be hard to tell what she was shouting *about*, though. She wouldn't be ordering somebody to do something. Nor was she complaining that they *hadn't* done whatever she wanted doing. She shouted when there was no one else around. It didn't make sense - unless she was shouting at *Mary*, who would be indoors.

Some things you never quite found out, and it may have been that the grown-ups of Elderberry Lane didn't know, either. But Mr Bailey had had to go to prison once, it was said. And not so very long ago. It was almost the worst thing that could happen to a family. What he had done wrong wasn't clear, though it had apparently been a serious matter.

So you had to wonder about the whole Bailey family, not just the daughter. But it was Mary who I was beginning for some reason to feel curious about. One day after school I asked Johnny about her. He was in a better position to know *something* at least, going to the same school.

"Mary Bailey? I've never spoken to her."

"Does anybody?"

"Sometimes, yes. Girls, anyway. But not very often, I suppose."

"Don't *you* wonder about her?"

He shrugged his shoulders. "She walks to and from school on her own, that's all I've noticed. We're not in the same class."

"What about at playtime?"

"She doesn't play football with the boys, if that's what you mean."

"But does she skip with the other girls, and stuff like that?"

"I don't know."

"Or does she hang around the playground on her own?"

"Well, I think she does *that* sometimes."

"Nothing more, though?"

"I don't think so."

Johnny seemed to know no more about Mary than I did. It was strange, when we both lived quite close to her. But there seemed to be no way of finding out anything more about the girl and I soon stopped thinking about her. She and her family were a puzzle, and I was willing now to leave it at that.

Not so Johnny. I was surprised when he mentioned Mary Bailey again, a week or so later.

"I've seen her skipping sometimes, with two other girls swinging the rope," he said. "You know, when they all chant those funny rhymes. But mostly she's on her own in the playground, just hanging about... There's something else, though. I've noticed she sometimes looks upset."

"Upset? *Why?*"

"I couldn't tell. No one seemed to be bothering her. I think she was upset for some other reason. Maybe nothing to do with school."

"What do you think it could be?"

Johnny shrugged his shoulders. "No idea."

I expected him to lose interest in Mary for sure now, but the next thing that happened was that I saw him walking home from school with her. It was something boys just didn't *do*. I couldn't ever imagine walking home with someone like Susan Granger, and although she had dark hair, Mary was almost as pretty. Later he talked to me again.

"She won't tell me what's wrong," he said.

"What does she *say*?"

"She doesn't even speak."

"Not at *all*?"

"No. You ask her something and she just doesn't say anything."

"Why do you walk with her, then?"

"I don't know."

But Johnny carried on walking with Mary - sometimes on the way to school as well. He was getting to be quite worried about her, I could see. As if he ought to try to *do* something about whatever was wrong. But she said nothing to encourage him.

"I think it's got something to do with her mum and dad," he said. "I'm going to try and find out."

So he started watching *them* more closely. They didn't talk to one another, or to anyone else, he reported. She shouted a lot, that was all. And they didn't even sit on a bus or walk home together. But these were things that everybody already knew, and Johnny was aware of that. He was starting to feel quite angry at not being able to get any nearer to the truth about poor Mary. Then one day he met Mr Bailey in the lane and walked up to him. The man tried to push past, but Johnny said he wanted to talk to him about Mary. He didn't answer. Instead he gave Johnny a big shove, pushing him over. Then he made his funny barking sound and just walked away.

The incident put the wind up Johnny, but it made him more worried about Mary than ever. He felt he had to try to protect her somehow. But there was no way he could help her when she got home and had to go in, and that was where the trouble seemed to be.

Then something else started to happen.

"She can't *walk* properly now," he told me.

"Mary? *Anybody* can walk."

"*She* can't. She was *limping* today."

"Maybe she's hurt her leg."

"I don't know. There was something *funny* about it… She seemed upset again, too. And she said she didn't *feel* very well."

I was pretty sure that Johnny was thinking her dad was responsible, but I suddenly had a different thought - a more *horrible* one. Pete had been telling me about this scary new illness. They were calling it *infantile paralysis*. A lot of children were getting it, he said. He'd read about it in the paper. They got so they couldn't move their arms and legs properly. Some couldn't even *breathe*. They had to be put in something called an *iron lung*.

But I didn't say anything about this to Johnny. I just hoped to hear that Mary had stopped limping and was all right again.

It didn't happen, though. Poor Mary got worse. She stopped going to school, and never appeared outdoors at all. We heard next that she'd gone into hospital. Then that she was out again. We saw ambulances, but we still didn't see Mary. Nobody was really talking to the family, but it was being said that she would soon be better. Then people said there was no hope for her. She was in an iron lung. Weeks passed, but no one really knew the truth.

Then there was talk that she'd been seen out of doors again with her mother, going to the house of an auntie down on the main road. It wasn't far, but Mary found it difficult, they said. I didn't see her myself for ages. I suppose I was usually at school when she came out. Then one summer's evening I *did* see her. From behind.

Her mother was almost having to hold her up. One of her shoulders seemed to be drooping badly, and her back was twisted somehow, and her legs weren't working properly. It was terribly sad, but I couldn't help being thankful that she couldn't see me, and that I wouldn't have to try to say anything.

After poor Mary got infantile paralysis she really did have no friends. Even Johnny stopped trying to talk to her.

11

OUR FAT

"What about David Sherburn?" Johnny said, when we were talking about the Quarry family one day.

"To fight *Fat*?"

It was certainly an idea - one we hadn't thought of before.

"How would we persuade him, though."

"Why don't we just *ask* him?"

"Might be worth a try."

Somebody was going to have to stand up to Fat. It was the only way of ending the rule of the Quarrys on Elderberry Lane. David wasn't one of the gang - much too superior for that - but he was probably our best hope.

The Quarrys ranged from near infants to full adults. With their red screwed-up faces and short blond hair they were different sizes of the same thing - all except for Fat, who had red hair, too. They called each other "Our This" and "Our That", and the rest of the neighbourhood kids usually talked about them in the same way.

The youngest was Our Jimmy. He was already a wicked little street fighter, even though he hadn't long been at school. Next, a few years older, came Our Barb. She had learnt at an early age that it was easy to fight boys because they were afraid of hitting a girl. *Really* hitting one, that is. She used a combination of thumps and slaps and kicks, and even *bites* when she wasn't winning. After Barb came Our Dennis, who was the same age as me. Then Our Sam - another girl, though it didn't make a lot of difference - followed by Our Mickey and, scariest of all, Our Fat himself. Beyond Fat, sort of held in reserve, though they were adults now, were Our Gert and, oldest of all, Our Bert. No one could remember when Bert had been anything but grown up.

Fat Quarry wasn't really fat. Not in the blubbery sense. *Beefy* would be the way to describe him. His clothes were tight fitting, his collar digging in around his red neck. You simply couldn't mess with Our Fat. Nobody had ever fought him. You felt it would be suicide. All previous wars with this rough family had ended with Our Mickey, who could fight pretty well everyone on Elderberry Lane himself.

But David Sherburn had never been tested. He was now a very good-looking young teenager with lustrous black hair and an athletic build, an only child from a posh family. They lived in a detached house standing back from the road, with a big, tree-shaded garden. They had a car, too. And a garage to keep it in. Everyone expected David Sherburn to grow up to be an important man. He was the only boy on Elderberry Lane to have passed for the grammar school so far.

His mum and dad bought him things that the other families couldn't afford. He had a sporty bike, with alloy handlebars and *derailleur* gears, his own football, which he barely used but kept well-dubbined, even his very own royal-blue football *kit*, with his initials *DS* stitched on the chest. He also had a tennis racquet, with a press, and his own cricket bat, ball and stumps. Then there were his two pairs of shiny red boxing gloves. He had never used them in a real boxing match, though - only for shadow boxing. I was aware of all this because some of us were allowed in, one at a time, to look at but never to touch these wondrous possessions.

There was always a rumbling war going on with the Quarrys. They lived way up at the top of Elderberry Lane and had to walk down if they were going anywhere at all. Usually, though, the war would be confined to intimidating glances, with occasional pushes and elbowings aside. If anyone stood up to them, at whatever level, there would always be an older brother or sister waiting to take revenge.

"You wait - I'll get Our Barb!" the challenged Quarry would cry. Or "Our Dennis!" or "Our Mickey!" - right up to Our Fat. And if anyone wanted to risk death by standing toe-to-toe with Our Fat, they might still have to face Our Bert - or even worse, Our *Gert*. Gert still had a reputation as a wicked street fighter like Barb, with nowadays the advantage of bigger muscles. One way or another, the Quarry family was definitely in control.

The latest trouble had begun right at the bottom of the heap.

Our Jimmy pushed little Malcolm Bailey, into a pile of soot, just for a laugh. They were about the same size, but it was no contest, and in any case everyone felt sorry for little Malcolm Bailey because his sister was so poorly. Weedy Barry Foster saw what happened and was brave for once. In fact he was quite a bit bigger than Jimmy Quarry and was able not only to push *him* into the soot, but to rub it into his hair and face, even his eyes. Jimmy came up blubbering and spitting.

"You wait!" he said. "I'll get Our Barb!"

When Barb Quarry next set eyes on Barry Foster she didn't bother with an argument but went straight on the attack.

Clumps of hair were pulled from his head, his shins were kicked and his face scratched until it was streaked with red. His big brother Keith found him sitting on the kerb, crying. Keith was just about old enough to stand up to Barb. He chased up the lane after the girl and caught her just as she reached her house.

Grabbing her by the hair, he swung her round, then pushed her to the ground with all his strength. She banged her head on the concrete gate post and blood appeared.

Unfortunately, just at that moment Our Dennis came out of their plywood front door. It took him only a second to size up the situation. Keith found himself running for *his* life. Dennis caught him and thumped him in as many places as he could think of. Poor Keith crumpled to the pavement. He told me later what had happened.

I was only just a bit bigger than Dennis. Knowing he would have to pass our front gate, I watched for him and took him by surprise, hurling him sideways across the road and through the thick privet hedge of the garden opposite. He was winded and scratched.

"You wait!" he snarled. "I'll get Our Sam!"

I was surprised. Usually they skipped to Mickey at this point. Sam wasn't as scary as Barb, but she was bigger, and still a Quarry. When she found me she squared up, crouching a bit, just like a boy. I didn't feel like fighting but landed a lucky punch on her lip. There was lots of blood. She backed off, wiping her mouth with the back of her hand.

"You've had it now!" she yelled. "I'll get Our Mickey!"

Avoiding him was impossible. One day he chased me on my bike and sent me flying into a wall. My knees were badly grazed.

Brian Darwent

I had to tell Pete about it.

Pete and Mickey were evenly matched. They wrestled furiously on a piece of cindery ground, first one on top and then the other. I watched from close by. When Mickey looked like winning I ran forward and tried to help, but Pete kicked me away. They'd fought before but he'd never managed to win. This time he was determined to make it different. On top again, he at last pinned Mickey's shoulders to the cinders and made him surrender. Mickey got slowly to his feet and threw a half-hearted final punch in the air before backing away.

"Our Fat'll be after you!" he told Pete.

Well, it took barely a word from Fat to scare the *life* out of poor Pete. He had only to wag a finger as he passed the gate. Although safe behind it, Pete didn't dare respond. He had to be very careful about venturing out for a while. All the fighting had been in vain, we realised. The Quarrys were still in charge.

It was then that our minds turned to David Sherburn.

David had already been the hero of Elderberry Lane once. We'd had a five-a-side rugby match against a team from across the main road, on a piece of waste land over there. In the other team were two brothers Jack and Danny Robinson, who were thought to be unstoppable. David had dealt with them with ease, however. He had his own effective way of tackling. He didn't go for the legs, but got them in a headlock whenever they threatened to score and wrestled them to the ground. Soon the two brothers were quickly passing the ball to avoid this undignified treatment. Elderberry Lane had won the match easily.

So when David invited me to have another look at all his sporty stuff one afternoon, I told him all about the latest trouble with the Quarry gang. He was fooling around in his red boxing gloves.

"Is *Fat* the problem?" he said.

"Mainly, yeah."

"And is everyone scared of him?"

"Who wouldn't be?"

"But why do you all think he's so tough?"

"Well - because he *is*."

"Has anyone ever fought him, though?"

"No, they wouldn't *dare*."

David had been shadow boxing a little as he spoke.

"Tell him I'll give him a proper fight," he said, suddenly punching the air more vigorously. "That's if he's *brave* enough."

Persuading him to take Fat on was turning out to be easier than I'd expected.

"A proper fight?"

"You know, with a boxing ring and referee and seconds and all that.

And boxing gloves as well. Like you see at the pictures sometimes. Think you and the other kids can organise it?"

"We'll *try*."

But Johnny saw a problem.

"Didn't he say he'd challenge Fat to a fight *himself*, face to face?" he asked later.

"No, that's definitely up to us, I think."

"So who's going to tell him about it?"

"I don't know."

"*You'll* have to tell him."

"Me? That's not fair! I've already persuaded David Sherburn to fight him. But I'd be too scared, anyway."

"What about *Pete*?"

"He'd be even more scared than me. Fat's still after him."

"Oh."

We tried to think who else might agree to take the message to Fat but there was nobody brave enough.

"You'll have to go back to David Sherburn, then." Johnny said. "Ask *him*. It's his fight."

"No, he'd change his mind. Fat would probably start a fight on the spot, without waiting for a boxing ring and everything."

"What can we do, then?"

We thought some more.

"I know," I said. "Let's put it in writing. I'll get Pete to help."

"But who would deliver it? It's the same problem."

"Let's *post* it."

There was no other way, so we talked to the rest of the gang and wrote a message to Fat. We didn't say who'd written it. It simply said:

> *DAVID SHERBURN CHALLENGES YOU TO A PROPER BOXING MATCH IN A BOXING RING ON KELLY'S BACK FIELD NEXT SATURDAY AFTERNOON AT 2 O'CLOCK.*
>
> *VEST, SHORTS AND GYM SHOES TO BE WORN. BOXING GLOVES WILL BE PROVIDED.*
>
> *BRING A SECOND.*
>
> *THE MARQUESS OF QUEENSBERRY RULES ARE TO BE OBSERVED.*

We'd got the last bit from Pete. In fact he helped with the whole thing.

Fat didn't write a reply. He simply got one of his brothers to tell us that he was definitely going to be there.

When Sunday afternoon came it was drizzling, which was probably as well as it meant that Kelly was unlikely to spoil things. I could picture him with his feet up at home, enjoying a large slice of his wife's homemade cake. We'd set up a makeshift ring with string ropes, and had two kitchen chairs we'd managed to borrow in the corners for the seconds. An older boy had been brought from outside the neighbourhood as referee, to ensure a fair fight. Someone had got hold of an ice-cream man's hand bell.

David Sherburn arrived in a blue vest with his initials on the front. He had his red boxing gloves on already. His second, a cousin, was carrying the pair intended for Fat. Ducking under the string ropes, David began to dance around the ring, breathing noisily and throwing shadow punches.

The rain didn't seem to be bothering him, we were glad to see. But where was his opponent?

Nobody had actually thought much about Fat, once he'd agreed to the fight. But when you stopped to think, it didn't seem likely that he'd be as well-equipped as David. The Quarrys were a very poor family. Nor was he going to be as eager to stick to the proper rules of boxing. We didn't know quite what to expect.

Well, when Fat Quarry did arrive at last he was alone and dressed in his everyday clothes. And it looked straight away as if the boxing match might turn out to be the shortest in history. He marched up to the ring and yanked at the string ropes until the corner posts fell down. Then, brushing aside the protests of the referee, he closed in on David, who had stopped dancing and seemed suddenly frozen to the spot. The boy with the bell stood ready, but he looked to be frozen, too.

No word was spoken. A single bare-knuckle blow to the jaw settled the matter.

David Sherburn would definitely have been out for the count if the referee hadn't been too dumbstruck to start one. His work done, Fat now strode away from the scene as purposefully as he'd arrived, leaving his opponent sprawled on the grass, his blue vest muddied. There were even tears in his eyes. The little group of damp spectators neither cheered nor booed. It surely meant that the Quarrys would be more in control than ever now.

But soon afterwards poor little Malcolm Bailey, who had helped to start all this, was messing about in the road one day when a fast car rounded the sharp bend at the bottom of Elderberry Lane. Fat Quarry happened to be walking by at that very moment. The hero that is in everyone was suddenly awakened. He dashed into the road and bundled the startled boy to safety, falling headlong as he did so. The driver swerved, but he couldn't avoid Fat's legs. Both were broken in several places.

After that - about six months afterwards - Fat could only walk with the help of a stick. Later he was able to do without it, but he still hobbled.

His running days were over, and to remain effective, street bullies need to be fast on their feet. So it was that the ultimate threat, which had kept the Quarry family in control in Elderberry Lane, was at last removed, although we still remained very wary of Our Gert for a long time after.

12
BONNY NIGHT

"What about that *big* one near the Ginnels? You seen that?"

Johnny Stone and I were sitting astride our old bikes, talking about bonfires we'd spotted - or *bonnies*, as we called them. Bonny Night, the most exciting night of the year for us, was getting close.

"Yeah, it's *massive*," I said. "Been right up to it?"

"No, them Ginnels' kids are real *scary*. Have you?"

"Yeah, I was riding by on my way to Auntie Jessie's shop one day when I noticed they'd got nobody guarding it, so I stopped and had a quick look."

Hardly anybody had a *new* bike - only David Sherburn, in fact - but they were still important to us. By now we practically lived on them, and we could ride them wherever we liked. Nobody worried much. Auntie Jessie kept a newagent's and general store in the rough part of town we called the Ginnels. I felt safe on my bike. Her shop protected me from the tough kids of the neighbourhood, but I knew I could always make an *attempt* to escape by racing there. She never seemed to close.

"What's it really *like*, that bonny?" Johnny asked.

"It's built of old planks and boxes and stuff. Couldn't see any tree branches at all. That's how eveyone's started building them now. Have you noticed?"

"Yeah, it's *cheating*. Bonnies are suppose to be built from *proper* wood."

That's what we believed on Elderberry Lane. We went out into the country with axes and saws and brought back fresh wood cut from living trees, like a successful hunting party returning proudly to camp. But this year it hadn't been so easy. We were being watched. The result was that we were miles behind with the building of our bonny - yet we still wanted it to be the biggest and best around.

Johnny gripped the brakes of his bike and bounced the front wheel in anger. "It's all *Bobby Howard's* fault," he said.

"Yeah, I know."

Bobby Howard was a grumpy old retired policeman with one eye who lived close to Johnny's house. No one liked him much, but he could make a lot of trouble still and was forever interfering in what we kids were up to, especially when Bonny Night was coming up. We never involved grown-ups, or even older kids if we could help it. We saw gathering wood and building the bonny - even *lighting* the fire on the big night - as *our* job.

We certainly didn't like old Bobby Howard sticking his nose in.

"Can't we just take no notice of him?" I said.

"Not after *last* year. My dad says we've definitely got to stop cutting branches from the trees in the hedgerows. Otherwise Bobby Howard will report us, he reckons."

"What are we going to *do* then? There isn't any old wood just lying about that we could use, even if we wanted to. Not *enough*, anyway."

"There's always Tommy Fairbrother's dark woods."

"We don't want to get *shot*."

Since the accident Tommy Fairbrother wasn't the farmer he'd once been, and his two scary sons had gone off into other lives by now, but we still felt it was risky to trespass on his land.

"We haven't got much time left, though."

"I know."

We both bounced our bikes for a bit.

"I wonder where they got all the wood for that big bonny?" Johnny said.

"*Stole* most of it, I expect."

There was another long silence, then he suddenly blurted out:

"Why don't we do the same? *Steal* some."

"What? … Where *from*?"

I was stunned for a moment. I hadn't meant to put that idea in his head.

"From other *bonnies*."

"But we can't do *that*!"

"Why not?"

"Well… we just *can't* It'd be *cheating*."

"You can bet your life that's what *they* did - the Ginnels' gang."

"Yeah, but…"

"I'll bet they're not the *only* ones, either."

This was probably true. We'd had stuff stolen from our bonny in the past, and it was happening more than ever now. It was the reason why other kids were taking no chances and guarding their bonnies. But I still wasn't keen on the idea.

"They'd *catch* us," I said.

"Not it they didn't *see* us. They won't have guards all night. We'll do it after it goes dark. That's pretty early now. And we'll only pinch as much as we can carry - from different bonnies on different nights. They mightn't even *notice*... There's no time left to do anything different, anyway."

I gave my bike a last bounce, but I stopped arguing. Johnny's idea sounded like a plan, at least. The only plan we had.

It didn't us take long to put the idea to other kids in the lane who usually helped with the bonny and round up a small gang. Keith Foster wanted to bring along his weedy brother, Barry, who was a crybaby and could be a nuisance, but we let it go. Everyone was scared but excited at the same time. We knew it would be easy enough to make the excuse at home that we would be staying out after dark in someone else's house, because no one had a telephone to check. Nor did we lose any time in racing around to all the best bonnies on our bikes to decide how best to approach them. Now all we had to do was carry out the plan.

Well, it was as easy as taking sweets off a baby, as the grown-ups sometimes said. Soon we were creeping back through the darkness to our bonfire site on Elderberry Lane with planks and crates and any other old timber we could carry. We even felt relaxed enough to spend time rearranging the stuff left at each of the bonnies to give the appearance that nothing had gone. In just a few nights we'd gathered enough wood to build a bonny that was at least the equal of most of those we'd stolen from, especially as they were now all a bit smaller. But we weren't quite satisfied. One last raid - a second visit to that big bonny near the Ginnels - ought to do it, we thought. They certainly had plenty left, even though we'd already taken more than we planned.

The moon was already up on a clear night when we set off. On the rare times when I was out at night I wondered about the moon and stars. And the sun in the daytime, too. Were they all inside or outside the glass sky? They looked to be *inside*, but then that made the sky seem so *very* far away that it was impossible to imagine... But this was no time to think for long about that stuff. Not that we were frightened, or even nervous so certain were we that this raid again would be dead simple. After a lot of stumbling about in the darkness, we had even got hold of a couple of torches. Nor did we much bother about the noise we were making. Most stupid of all, though, we weren't allowing for the strong likelihood that by now word of what we were up to would have spread around.

So they were ready for us - some of the scariest kids in the whole of the world, as we saw them. They waited in silence until we'd got ourselves greedily weighed down with the stuff we were pinching, then slipped out of hiding, like shadows in the night. We barely saw the fists that were soon flying. In a very short time we were moaning in the mud, like wounded soldiers on a battlefield.

But thankfully they didn't seem to want to kill us altogether. Instead they appeared to forget us as they set about painstakingly rebuilding their wrecked bonny. And hurt as we were we could see in the moonlight how much it *meant* to them

- a thing built with their own hands, to be the envy bonfire-builders everywhere.

Somehow, empty handed, we managed to stagger off home. But it was only when we reached Elderberry Lane again that we realised one of our gang was missing. In the confusion, we'd left Keith Foster's weedy brother Barry behind.

Well, we could imagine only too easily what the Ginnels' kids might do with him - use him for their *Guy*, most likely! They could be *that scary*!

They didn't seem to have one in place, and making a Guy was always a bit of a nuisance for Bonny Night, so a ready-made one would be a bonus for them.

"Come home with me to explain," pleaded Keith.

Like the rest of us, Keith knew where their back-door key was hidden, and would normally have let himself in the back way. But instead he knocked timidly on his own front door. No one answered, so he had no choice but to knock louder - and at last his dad appeared.

At first he was puzzled.

"What's this?" he said. "*Carol singers?*" "A bit early for that!"

Then he saw who we were and the state we were in. We bent our heads and stared miserably at the ground.

"It wasn't our *fault*," Keith blurted out.

"That's right," someone else said. "We got *attacked*."

"And we hadn't even *done* anything," put in another voice.

"We *tried* to escape."

"There were too *many* of them."

"We did our best to fight back, but they were too *big* as well."

"Then we managed to run for it. *Most* of us."

Keith's dad said something at last:

"*Most* of you?"

He surveyed the dirty faces, some streaked with blood.

"Where's our *Barry*?" he shouted.

"They've *got* him... We think they may be planning to use him for the Guy on their bonny."

"*Who's* got him? Where *was* this?"

"In the Ginnels, Mr Foster. Near that big bonfire."

"The *Ginnels*!"

Mr Foster could be a very angry man. Most of the time he was as calm and reasonable as you could want, but underneath we knew he had a violent temper. Just like lots of fathers, in fact. We half expected to get beaten up afresh - the lot of us.

But he ducked inside to grab his coat.

"Come on!"

So we set off with torches again for the big bonny near the Ginnels, Mr Foster striding out in the lead. And luckily a few of the gang were still hanging around in the darkness. We could just make out Barry. He was over to one side - sitting on a box, crying quietly. They were leaving him alone for now but you could tell that, like a cat with a mouse, if he dared move they would be ready to pounce.

His dad hadn't yet noticed him. He marched up to the biggest of the gang, their leader, who really *was* a bully - a lad called Garrity. We didn't know his first name, if he had one. He had a tattoo on his arm and used every swear word there was. We'd had trouble with him before.

"Where's my *son*?" demanded Mr Foster.

"*I* don't know," Garrity sneered.

"Then let me try and help you *think*!"

Mr Foster lifted him into the air and shook him violently. It was the last thing the bully was expecting. He shrieked, struggling to free himself, and pointing desperately at Barry. Mr Foster dropped him like a sack of rubbish, and a moment later he'd vanished with the rest of the gang into the night.

Making our way back, Mr Foster said he thought the whole business was serious enough for the police to be contacted. He told us he would call at the station the very next day. We were quietly glad. It made it easier for the rest of us to go home. When they saw our torn clothes and cuts and bruises, and we explained how we'd been the innocent victims of a violent attack - which Mr Foster intended reporting - our mums and dads were straight away on our side.

And so too were the police when they called. They weren't very interested when we confessed that we'd stolen a little bit of wood from the Ginnels' kids bonfire. They were always in trouble and had probably pinched most of the stuff themselves. The violent attack was more serious, though. But then no one had been *badly* hurt, had they? And as for Barry Foster, well, he hadn't been *kidnapped*, had he? When they saw the kids again they'd give them a cuff around the ears, the policemen promised. That was all that would be needed. It was all a bit of a storm in a teacup really.

But that wasn't the end of it. The *Reporter* somehow got hold of the story. They made a bit of a thing about the way rival gangs were stealing one another's bonfire wood. But what interested the newspaper far more was the *size* of the bonfire the Ginnels' lads had built. Someone had been sent out to investigate other bonnies and they hadn't been able to find a bigger one. *Their* bonfire was the biggest for miles around. So the rough, tough kids of the Ginnels had their photographs taken standing in front of their creation, and the story was printed on the front page.

As for our own bonny that year, we found ourselves back where we started because while we were preoccupied with these other things most of the stuff we'd stolen was stolen *back*. But then old *Bobby Howard* of all people came unexpectedly to our rescue. It turned out that he had really wanted to help us all along. He'd kept a great stack of old timber with our bonny in mind after rebuilding some fencing, though he insisted we could only have it if we let *him* light the fire. And he'd been busy, too, making a simple Guy for us in his garden shed out of stuffed old sacks. It had a slight look of Garrity, the leader of the Ginnels' gang. Or at least we *pretended* it had as it went up in flames on Bonny Night.

13

THE OLD MAN IN THE COUNTRY

We'd heard the rumours, we kids on Elderberry Lane, but no one could be sure about him. The old man, rarely sighted, was like a country ghost. Nobody ever seemed to get more than a glimpse of him, always distant and always the back view, walking slowly away, his face unseen, soon to disappear into the mist or among the trees. He wore a cap, they said, and a whiteish raincoat. He might also walk with a stick.

Keith Foster's Uncle George had told him that the old man might really *be* a ghost. Uncle George, who had a bad limp and spoke in a loud whisper when he was talking to kids - looking away as if he wasn't really speaking to them - was always telling us scary things anyway, so I didn't believe it. But *Keith* did. The old man was an old soldier, Uncle George said, who'd been left to wander the earth after his mates, also killed, had gone to heaven. That happened sometimes, he reckoned, if too many men died at the same time. He was talking about young men killed in the earlier world war - the one our grandfathers had fought in. That war was still a painful memory for many older people. A lot of men *hadn't* been killed, but had returned home badly wounded - more than in the recent war, the one *we* knew all about. Uncle George's whispered advice, for anyone willing to listen, was that we should stay away from this old country wanderer, man *or* ghost.

Billy Stringer had heard a different rumour, though one that also had to do with war and injury. Such things were never far from people's minds. Ever since the car-painting episode Billy's dad had tried to make him stay away from Elderberry Lane, but it wasn't working any more, even though Billy was really frightened of him. There just weren't enough kids down on the main road for him to hang around with. *His* rumour, anyway, was that the old man had a horrible war wound of some sort, which forced him to stay away from people so he wouldn't scare them to death.

We were becoming like Pete. We'd get obsessed with things - or people - and lately it was this old man. Why we hadn't thought about him before, I don't know.

"He can't be a *ghost*," I said. "There's no such thing."

It was a mild day in winter and we were up on the stone railway bridge, Keith, Billy and me. Right at the top of Elderberry Lane, way past the Quarrys' house and slicing through the American base, there was a railway line in a deep cutting. The railway bridge, like any other, was a magnet for us. We liked to try, through the smoke, to drop sods of earth down the funnels of the steam trains as they passed below. Or climb the fence and creep down to the rails themselves to position ha'pennies on them in the hope of having them transformed into pennies. But mostly we just hung about there, talking.

"He *is* a ghost, though," said Keith. "Uncle George knows what he's talking about."

"Since when? He just talks that way to scare us."

"No, he knows his stuff. You can ask him about practically anything and he knows the answer."

"What does he *do*, anyway?"

"He doesn't work. He's got a bad leg since the war, so he can't. He borrows lots of library books and sits and reads all day long. That's why he knows so much."

"Anyway, there's no such thing as ghosts," I insisted. "Something that isn't always there can't *be* there. It's dead simple."

"Who told you that?"

I hesitated.

"Well, it was Pete. But he knows what *he's* talking about, too."

"Yeah, but he's really only a kid still. Uncle George has been grown up for years. He was practically grown up before the *war.*"

Billy wasn't listening much to this. He was on the lookout for his dad.

Mr Stringer, though quite posh, was tall and muscular - and with a vicious temper, too. Even worse than *Keith's* dad's. If he caught Billy not only in Elderberry Lane but way up near the base and the railway, and with one of the kids who'd painted his precious car, he'd give him a good hiding while we all watched. Billy was getting to be much too big for that sort of treatment, but his dad would do it anyway. What's more, he often came looking for him. But Billy was listening enough to join in the argument just a little.

"He's got a wound, like my *granddad* says. That's all."

"Does your granddad know him?" asked Keith "I don't know. I don't think so. He knows *about* him, though… But in any case, how could a ghost get to be old?"

"Yeah, you'd think a ghost would still look young, like when the man died," I said, backing up Billy. "That's if it existed at all."

"Ghosts can grow old, too, I bet," said Keith. "I'll ask Uncle George about that. He'll know."

We stopped talking then. We'd spotted something...

A farm track from the bridge led in the direction of a small wood. One of the funny things about this wood was that it was almost perfectly round. The other was that in winter it was full of tightly curled-up hedgehogs - whether hibernating or dead, you couldn't tell. A kind of hedgehogs' graveyard, perhaps. But close to the wood now we'd spotted a moving figure. It looked to be wearing a whiteish raincoat and cap, and was tilted slightly as well, as if leaning on a stick. But as we screwed up our eyes to try to make out if it might really be the ghostly old man, the figure disappeared from view.

There was a path right around the circular wood, so if we waited for a while he might reappear, we thought - the path didn't lead anywhere else. But he would be too far away still for us to get a proper look at him. And why wait? If we raced to the wood we'd be in time to hide in the bushes before he came around. And then the mystery would at last be solved.

I wanted to do this, but Keith and Billy were less keen. So I told them quickly what *I'd* heard - which was less scary.

"He's keeping out of his *wife's* way," I told them. "They can't stand one another. He's too old to work and doesn't like to be seen wandering the streets, so he walks in the country, that's all. But I still want to be sure."

Keith said he still believed Uncle George, though.

"Just us two, then?" I said to Billy. I was a bit scared myself to go and investigate the matter alone.

But Billy was looking over my shoulder to see if his dad was coming up the lane yet to find him. And he suddenly let out a little cry. I turned and saw Mr Stringer, in the far distance. You could still tell that he was in a furious mood, however.

"Quick, let's run before he *sees* us!" I said.

Keith didn't wait. Instead of dashing in the direction of the wood, though, he jumped over the railway fence to hide *under* the bridge.

"*Come on!*" I yelled at Billy.

But it was too late. He was frozen to the spot. Then he began to do a frightened little dance as his father got closer.

I definitely didn't want to stay and watch poor Billy being given his good hiding. It was no fun to watch. So I began to run myself - and there was only one way to go. Towards the wood.

The old man still hadn't reappeared. I must have run quicker than I'd ever done in my life, reaching the wood in an amazingly short time. I thought for a moment of Jesse Owens and his records, but I had no time for that. Careful not to kneel on any hedgehogs, I settled in the bushes.

I only had to wait a few moments before I heard the slow tread of someone approaching. I held my breath as the mysterious figure came into view. Then I stood up. I don't know why.

He wasn't a ghost at all. He was an old man in a whiteish raincoat and cap, leaning on a stick, just as everyone had said.

But no sooner had I made myself visible than he turned to face me, a look of rage and pain in his eyes. He raised the stick and stepped forward.

I tried to tell him I was only looking for hibernating hedgehogs. We were doing hibernation at school. But no sound came out. I hung on for a moment, feeling ashamed somehow. Then I turned and fled.

The old man had no nose.

14

BABY GRAHAM

I sometimes wondered why my Auntie Jessie, my only remaining favourite auntie now, still lived in the Ginnels, the rough area of tiny back-to-back terraces, cobbled streets and ragged, often shoeless kids, a mile or so from Elderberry Lane. You didn't feel safe there. Everyone else in the family - even my gran - had managed to get out long ago. But Auntie Jessie hadn't made it.

She was big woman with hair that had been grey for as long as I could remember, yet she was a good soul, everyone said, who managed to stay cheerful in spite of the hard life she had to lead in that tough part of town. You felt she was meant for better things. My mum blamed her wastrel husband, Uncle Sid, a lanky, sharp-faced man with a moustache and a cap on his head day and night. Auntie Jessie was *punished*, my mum often said. I wondered for what, until I realised that she hadn't done anything wrong. She was punished by *life*.

There was a small framed photograph on our sideboard of my mum and dad's wedding. Auntie Jessie stood at my dad's shoulder, almost towering over him, in her old-fashioned bridesmaid's dress and bonnet.

She was nothing like my Auntie Kate, also in the picture. You'd never have guessed they were sisters.

Her shop was close to the main road through the Ginnels, though there weren't many passing cars, even now. Besides selling papers and magazines she had fancy stuff in her small window. It was never very eye-catching, however. I don't think she really expected to *sell* any of it. She just liked to dream of the day when someone might stop by in a car. A car was so far beyond Auntie Jessie's dreams that she thought anybody who owned one must be practically royalty.

The little newsagents shop was also the family house - Jessie and Sid and their son Tom - when he was at home. Once they'd lived a few doors away. When the shop came up for sale she'd believed it was going to be a big step up in the world for them.

"Sid seemed as keen to buy it as she was," I'd heard my mum once say. "He was mainly interested in seeing the betting tips in all the papers every morning, though. Never lifted a finger to help. He was down at that *nursery* place all day long. Never had a proper job."

As for their Tom, he was older even than Pete and would soon be leaving school - not that he often went - and ready to start work. But the idea of getting a proper job hadn't occurred to *him*, either. He spent *his* time down at the nursery now. I never knew why they called it that. It was just a ramshackle allotment. They certainly never grew anything there, though there were a few hens and ducks wandering about the place, and sometimes the odd pig. Tom had been buying and selling them since he was very young and had by now more or less taken the place over from his dad, who was supposed to be busy with other things. He even had a sort of *home* down there - a shed, really - with a few bits of furniture, and had taken to living there most of the time. Auntie Jessie disapproved, but with all her other worries and problems she didn't seem to be able to do much about it. Tom had a dream, though. He loved horses and intended one day to open a riding school.

Mostly Auntie Jessie relied on local urchins for delivering the papers. She had no choice. They could just about be trusted to push the right newspapers through the right letterboxes, but letting them handle money wasn't safe. That's where she hoped *I* might come in, young as I was. I could maybe collect the money for her on Sunday mornings. In fact it was my gran who arranged the job, and she was someone you couldn't argue with. Besides, Pete had done it for a while and now it was my turn. I liked the idea of earning a bit of money, but those cobbled streets in the Ginnels were dangerous.

I wasn't a good collector, not really feeling big enough to be doing such a job, for one thing. Walking about with a little bag with money in it was no fun. I was also too scared to keep knocking at the doors of the more difficult houses, while I hardly dared knock at all at the impossible ones. Auntie Jessie never complained as she gave me my two shillings wages, though. She couldn't afford to lose me.

One day, when I had been doing the job for about six months, my mum told me something very strange. Auntie Jessie had had a baby. Not that she was *going* have a baby, but that she had already *had* it. Then she said that the baby's name was Graham and that it wouldn't live for more than six months.

I didn't ask any questions - I could see that Mum was upset - but it was baffling. Auntie Jessie hadn't got very fat, the way Auntie *Kate* had when she was expecting Baby Jack. At least I hadn't noticed anything. Nor had there been any talk of her going into hospital. And you couldn't possibly imagine that she and Uncle Sid had been getting up to the weird stuff in bed that Pete had described. Not at *their* age. I felt embarrassed again, even so. But there was also the scary thought that Baby Graham doomed to die almost before he'd even lived. On top of everything else, that was too much for me.

The only thing was to pretend to be ill. On the next Sunday morning I stayed in bed late, groaning a bit. Mum kept feeling my forehead and looking for spots. In fact she *kept* me in bed, so I didn't have to pretend any more. But my forehead must have stayed cool, and no spots came and I got very bored - so I was soon on my feet once more, without an excuse to stay away from Auntie Jessie's shop any longer.

Standing at the counter again, I felt myself blushing. It was as much as I could manage by way of a question about the baby. Auntie Jessie didn't notice, though. She simply gave me the little money bag, notebook and pencil without a word. I thought she looked upset, but I couldn't ask her about that, either. Then Uncle Sid bawled something from the parlour and she bawled something back, so I set off on my round.

It was the same for several weeks, and I began to think I must have misheard my mum. Then a Sunday morning came when she seemed a little brighter than usual, probably because Uncle Sid had gone down to the nursery or somewhere.

"Would you like to come in and see Baby Graham?" she asked. For all the difficulty of her life, she had quite a nice speaking voice.

I couldn't answer, but felt I had no choice but to push through the heavy curtain into the parlour. The place as usual was a shambles. They had a yard at the back, but rubbish of all kinds seemed to accumulate in Auntie Jessie's parlour, which was the only room they had for living in, the front room serving as the shop. There would even be junk on the *table* which at eating times had to be pushed harder against the wall to make space. She was meant to live better, but had given up the struggle long ago.

She led me through the debris and up the dark narrow staircase to the tiny bedrooms. And in the smallest and gloomiest there was a very small baby, lying on its stomach in a cot.

"This is Baby Graham," she said quietly, as if she didn't want to wake him. I expected her to pick the baby up, but she said she couldn't, or was afraid to, though she must have managed it somehow at feeding times. Then she told me that he would only live for six months. He had to lie on his stomach all the time because of a lump on his back.

"They say it's something called *spina bifida*," she said. "I don't know. It could break your heart, though. It really could."

I felt much too scared to feel properly sorry. Instead I found myself wondering why she'd bothered giving the baby a name, and why she'd chosen a sissy one like *Graham*. But at least I had the sense not to ask questions like that.

"I'm very sorry," was the best I could manage by way of comfort, in a voice that sounded terribly false to me.

Auntie Jessie never seemed to have much help in caring for her stricken child. My mum and dad were good people, as was my gran, though she was rather housebound by now. But women had to cope alone with the tragic side of life. I had to keep on visiting the shop every Sunday morning, more nervous than ever, wondering if the baby was still alive and unable to ask.

Then one day I knew that Baby Graham had died. I don't

know if he lived for exactly six months - that was the sort of information people took too literally. Nor do I know *how* I knew it had happened, because no one had yet mentioned it to me. I could just tell.

15

THE GIRL ON THE BIKE

I was at the seaside, beside the sea. It was the summer before I was due to start grammar school. Pete had been there for ages, though it hadn't changed him much. We were staying at the holiday camp in the resort with Mum. Dad was back at home. He had chickens now to take care of. You couldn't get close to the sea. That would have meant leaving the camp and it was against the rules, or something. But there was a grassy hill near our chalet with a seat, and you could see the sea from there. I was ill - properly this time, with a sore throat - but I was allowed now to sit up there, after spending two days in bed. Swallowing was still painful, though. The camp doctor had called and had given me a course of the new *M&B* tablets. My mum had insisted on it. They were a wonder drug that would cure all illnesses, everyone was saying. But I wasn't feeling any better yet. Quite woozy still, in fact. It was the tablets, apparently. I was too tired even to sketch.

The horizon stretched almost over the full width of the view before me. Half asleep, I gazed at it for a long time before I began to think at all.

Mum had gone off somewhere with Pete. He would be rowing on the boating lake, most likely, while she sat watching. Or maybe hanging around the outdoor swimming pool. He'd told me all about that. You could see girls in *bikinis*, he'd said.

Something about the horizon was puzzling me, in a dreamy sort of way. I couldn't think what it was. I hadn't seen it before, or at any rate hadn't noticed it. Not at the seaside. Then I realised what was bothering me. The horizon, which had to be the point where the sky and sea met, was too *near*. You felt you'd be able to sail out in a boat and reach it quite quickly. And yet the *sky* still looked as far away as ever. In fact you couldn't help wondering if it was really there. The blueness didn't look to be solid. Maybe there *was* no blue-glass surface. Maybe the sky and sea *didn't* meet at some very distant point, in the way I had always believed. The more I gazed, in fact, the more I couldn't help thinking that they didn't meet at all. How could they, if the sky didn't exist?

And then, still half in a dream, I noticed something else about the sea. It wasn't even flat. The surface of the sea was *curved*… You could see that quite easily, right there before your eyes… There was an horizon because the sea curved away from you so that you couldn't see it any more. And the surface of the *land* was curved, too, although that wasn't so obvious… I suddenly had the strangest feeling of being just a tiny, tiny creature, sitting on an enormous ball, or globe.

So *that's* what Pete had meant when he said the world was round.

It was funny that I could remember still, it was so long ago. Johnny Stone and I had had an argument about it. It meant that when in my mind I'd been spending the time since then *inside a* glass globe, really I'd been on the *outside* all along. And it was solid, and certainly not made of glass.

All through the time when Gus the Yank had brought Oscar to our house in the hope of meeting Angela, and we'd painted Billy Stringer's dad's old car bright orange, and I'd been smacked by stupid old Miss Nearhoof for fighting with girls when I hadn't done it, and Pete had sneaked out very early to investigate the Sunday morning gunshots, and we'd caught some leeches and so nearly put them cruelly to death, and Pete had had his own Olympic Games on Kelly's field, and Fat Quarry had beaten David Sherburn in a boxing match with a single punch, and we'd stolen wood for the bonny and got caught by the Ginnells' gang, and the *terrible* things that had happened as well - through all that time, until this moment, sitting on a hilltop seat at a holiday camp, I'd believed that's where I was. That's where we *all* were. Inside a glass globe that had never even existed...

Well, It was a bit too much to take in when you were feeling tired and ill... I couldn't help yawning... How come the people who lived on the other side of the globe didn't fall off?... Or for that matter why didn't we just float off into space, whatever space was?... And why was the sky *blue* when it wasn't even there?... I yawned again, then I fell asleep.

If the *M&B* tablets were working, they were working slowly. I was finding it hard to enjoy the week's holiday. Pete took me on the boating lake and rowed me around and in between the little islands. But I liked best riding on the two-seater, four-wheel bicycle contraptions. You sat side by side, sort of low down near the ground, and you both were supposed to pedal. I only pretended to, though. I just let my feet go round without putting any effort into it. Pete kept looking at me, then at my feet, but he didn't say anything.

I tried telling him about my discovery that the world was round after all, just like he'd told me long ago.

"I don't remember that," he said.

"You know - Johnny and I argued about it."

"About what?"

"About whether it was round or flat."

"What - the world?"

"Yeah."

"Everyone *knows* it's round."

"They don't. Not in the way you meant."

"How *else* could it be round?"

"It could be round and flat at the same time."

"But that's impossible."

"No it isn't. It could be *hollow*, with the land across the middle."

"What?"

"We'd be *inside* it, looking up at the sky."

"We look up at the sky *now*, don't we?"

"Not in the way I mean. It would be made of glass, or something. Sky-blue coloured."

"Made of *glass*? The world?"

But I just couldn't try and explain it any longer. Pete wasn't really interested. I was beginning to understand why, too. As we went along he was looking all the time at the girls we were passing. That was one way he *had* changed. We hadn't seen so many in one place before. Nothing *like* so many.

"Did you see *that* one?" he'd say. Or just, "*Wow!*"

And all roads seemed to lead back to the swimming pool. Pete would slow right down when we were near it, looking at the girls in their swimming costumes. Once he even whistled. But they looked more like women to me, the ones he was most interested in. He was disappointed that none of them were wearing bikinis.

"What's a bikini, anyway?" I asked him.

"It's to show off their figures."

Well, at least I knew what a *figure* was. Mum had said Auntie Kate had a good one, before she had Baby Jack.

"But *how*?"

"It's in two small bits - one to cover up the top part and the other the bottom. But they only really wear them in beauty contests."

"You mean like in the newsreels at the pictures?" I'd always found all that a bit boring, at least until now.

"Yeah, that's right. And guess what? There's a beauty contest right here at the pool tomorrow afternoon."

"Will *we* be able to watch it?"

"We *should* be. Everything's supposed to be free."

"What about Mum?"

"She told me *she* wanted to see it. It was her idea to go, and she'll want us to be with her."

So next day the three of us sat waiting in deckchairs by the pool. I was in a sulky mood. I was sure it was going to be boring, and my wooziness from the *M&B* tablets hadn't yet gone away completely.

Before the beauty contest started, one of the men you saw in red jackets told jokes loudly through a microphone, putting the audience in a happy, relaxed mood. He himself said that that was the idea, though it sort of annoyed me because I was having trouble *understanding* the jokes. They were different from the ones we heard at school, which were usually about an Englishman an Irishman and a Scotsman, and very funny. Pete was smirking to himself and stealing glances at me, meanwhile, but it wouldn't have surprised me if *he* wasn't understanding the jokes, either.

I didn't know about Mum.

The man asked for applause for the people who were to judge the contest next, and they each took a seat. One or two of them had been on the wireless. Then it was time for him to introduce the girls themselves, one by one.

He called them girls, but they were certainly a lot older even than Pete. They each carried a number. They walked slowly along the side of the pool and then stopped at a certain point, turning to smile briefly at different parts of the audience. Some had pretty smiles, while others had smiles that weren't so nice. They were mostly wearing one-piece bathing suits, though a few were in bikinis. One of these, in a pink bikini with white spots, you couldn't *help* looking at. It was the way she walked, somehow swaying slightly. And the sort of figure she had. She had the nicest *smile* of all, too, and when she paused for a moment to smile at the audience she looked directly at us. I couldn't help looking away for a second. I was starting to turn red. Pete gave me a quick glance again.

The girls had to chat into the microphone with the man running the show, and the girl we couldn't take our eyes off had the loveliest voice as well. At the end they all walked in procession back along the side of the pool and disappeared from view. There could only be one winner.

Mum said she was pleased with the result when it was announced, because it had gone to the girl with the nicest smile and the pleasantest manner. Pete looked happy, too, as the girl in the spotted bikini stepped once more out of the shadows to have the winner's gold sash slipped around her neck. Then he whispered something to me.

"*What?*" I whispered back.

Mum had stood up with the rest to clap while the girls were doing a final parade along the side of the pool.

"Did you see her *wink* at me? I'll tell you more about it later…"

So, sitting on the seat with the sea view later, while Mum was out playing bingo, Pete told me more.

"I *know* her," he said. "That's why she winked."

"But she *didn't* wink. *I* didn't see her do it."

"You weren't watching, and she was very subtle about it."

"What does *that* mean - subtle?" Besides being tired still, I was also feeling angry for some reason.

"It means she winked in a way that no one else would notice."

"Anyway, how do you know her? You *can't* do."

"I've seen her near the pool, while I was riding around on my own. When you were ill."

"But that isn't the same as *knowing* her."

"I know where she *lives*."

"What? Which *town* she lives in, you mean?"

"No - her chalet number."

"So you followed her back?"

"No, I just happened to be passing one day and saw her hanging out some washing on a line."

"People don't do washing on holiday."

"*She* does."

"Anyway, *that* isn't knowing her, either."

"She asked me the time, though."

"Asked you the time? You haven't even got a *watch*."

"I know. But I was able to stop and talk to her - for *twenty minutes*, at least."

"What about? Why would she want to talk to *you*?"

"Maybe she *likes* me."

"But you don't even *know* her."

"Yes I do. She blew me a kiss as well, as I was riding off. Honest to God! And then she winked at me today, when she was in the middle of the beauty contest... She's the most beautiful girl I've ever seen."

"But she isn't a girl. She's a *woman*."

"Well, the man with the microphone called her a girl."

This was just like the old Pete. You half suspected he was making it all up. *More* than half suspected. But this time I was really fed up of it. Instead of asking more questions I stood up and slouched off down the grassy hill, leaving him open-mouthed for once.

Back home a few weeks later I saw a girl ride past on a bike. Or maybe she was a woman, it was hard to tell. She looked very nice, anyway, with no make-up that you could see, wearing a pretty summer dress. On her shoulder was a small black bag. You would have said that she was simply out enjoying a ride on a sunny afternoon. Nothing more. The trouble was, she was riding slowly in the direction of the American base.

There were still plenty of Yanks up there, even though the war had been over for so long. And although they were usually hard to spot, deep inside the big flash American cars, sometimes you saw women *walking* up Elderberry Lane to meet them - women in high heels with *lots* of make-up. *Tarts*, Mum called them. They were the reason why she herself wouldn't wear lipstick. These tarts were Pete's latest obsession. You never saw one on a *bike*, though.

I didn't realise he'd seen this particular girl until he appeared at my side from nowhere.

"Wonder where *she's* off to?" he said.

"Who, that girl on the bike?"

"Yeah. I reckon she isn't as innocent as she looks."

"She's just out riding. What's wrong with that?"

"You *bet* she is! She's a *tart*, I'd say. I'm going to follow her and find out." And with that he brought out his own bike and set off slowly up the lane in pursuit.

I'd been on my way to Johnny's house, but hesitated. I couldn't help wondering about the girl myself. If Pete was right, you just couldn't believe it. She was just an ordinary girl out for a bike ride, surely...

But *was* she?

I couldn't move. I wanted to carry on to Johnny's. Then I thought it would be best to go back in. But I couldn't get the girl out of my mind riding so innocently in the direction of all those Yanks, who at times were so desperate to know if you had an older sister.

It was a long struggle, but finally I set off on foot up the lane myself, though only at a snail's pace. I'd walked quite a distance, even so, when I saw Pete racing back down the lane. When he reached me he skidded to a halt.

"What's *happened?*" I had to ask.

"I saw it all," he said. "The Yanks were lying on the grass as usual, reading comics - you know, where I used to talk to Gus. But they got to their feet when they spotted her. *Five or six* of them."

"She didn't stop, though, did she?"

"Yeah. She got off and stood with her bike, having a conversation with them. I was hiding behind a tree."

"What were they talking about? Could you hear?"

"No, but you can bet it was about *money.*"

"So what happened after that?"

"After they'd talked for a bit she leant her bike against a fence post and they pulled up the wire to help her get through."

"*Then* what happened?"

"They took her into one of the huts and closed the door."

"What, all *five or six* of them?"

"Yeah. Maybe more than that. Honest to God!"

"But for how long?"

"Oh, not all *that* long. When I saw the hut door start to open again I beat it… I expect she'll be coming back this way soon."

And precisely at that moment the girl on the bike reappeared over Pete's shoulder. She still looked perfectly fresh and neat to me as she rode slowly by, without a hair out of place. A picture of innocence, you would have said - almost like a girl in an Ovaltine advert - except maybe for that little black shoulder bag…

But no, I wasn't having any of it. It wasn't that I had no interest in what the Yanks got up to with the women who visited the base. I hadn't been able to stop myself following him. But I refused to believe a word of what our Pete had said about the girl on the *bike*. Not one single word.

———————

ABOUT THE AUTHOR

Brian Darwent is the author of a biography of the writer Jack Trevor Story (of *The Trouble with Harry/Live Now, Pay Later* fame). Stephen Fry described it as "a wonderful book about an extraordinary and deeply unusual writer and man", while Byron Rogers, in a full-page *Guardian* piece, called it "a little comic classic". He has also been involved in reviving William Saroyan's stories, and had a hand in several anthologies, two of them published in America. His own stories often appear in small-press literary magazines.

I wanted to remind older people what they once were.

Mark Twain
(on being asked if *Tom Sawyer* was really a children's book)

Available worldwide from Amazon
and all good bookstores

———————————

www.mtp.agency

www.facebook.com/mtp.agency

@mtp_agency

Michael Terence
Publishing